BREAK POINT

"I held the lift for you."

Maria noticed that the door to the lift was propped open by a tennis racket. But the lift itself had gone, leaving a black hole in its wake.

"It doesn't seem to have worked," Maria said, reaching forward to press the call button. Her companion leaned forward – to remove the racket, Maria thought. But then she felt a hand pressing firmly against her back.

"Hey, wha—?"

Maria was propelled forward, into the lift shaft. She screamed, but her cries went unheard, as the doors closed above her and the tennis star crashed on to the concrete floor, ten flights below.

Other titles in the Point Crime series:

Look out for:

POINT CRiME

BREAK POINT

David Belbin

■SCHOLASTIC

Scholastic Children's Books
7–9 Pratt Street, London NW1 0AE, UK
a division of Scholastic Publications Ltd
London ~ New York ~ Toronto ~ Sydney ~ Auckland

First published by Scholastic Publications Ltd, 1995

ISBN 0 590 55931 1

Typeset by TW Typesetting, Midsomer Norton, Avon

Printed by Cox & Wyman Ltd, Reading, Berks.

10 9 8 7 6 5 4 3 2 1

For Sue, again

1

FRENCH OPEN

Prologue

M aria Hernandez turned on the TV in her hotel suite. Conveniently, it was already tuned to the Sports Channel. When you were the world number one, even the tiniest details were taken care of. The picture came first, showing Maria's closest rival, an attractive fair-haired Australian. Maria turned the sound up and got a shock.

"...has announced her withdrawal from the French Open. Ms Murray's doctor told reporters that the world number two has injured her shoulder in a traffic accident and needs surgery. She may be out of the game for up to a year."

Maria didn't know whether to laugh or cry. She and Sue Murray weren't friends, but their fierce rivalry was more intense than most friendships. Each had beaten the other eleven times. Sue Murray was the only player who came close to Maria. Without her, the tournament at Roland Garros would be a walk-over. Maria would get bored. The press would get bored. Then the public would get bored. It all meant less money coming into the sport. Sue's accident was a disaster.

Maria picked up the telephone. She would find out where Sue was staying and send her the biggest bouquet of flowers available. But before she could dial room service, there was a familiar knock on the door. The knock was that of her father, who travelled with her everywhere. Usually, his knock was accompanied by a wisecrack in Spanish, but today, just the knock. He was probably as pre-occupied with Murray's health as she was. Maria wondered what kind of accident had befallen the Australian girl.

"It's open," she said softly. "Come in."

But the person who came into the room wasn't her father. The similarity of the knocks must have been coincidence.

"Oh," Maria said, turning down the sound on the TV. "I thought you were someone else."

"Your father asked me to get you. There's an immediate press conference downstairs about the Sue Murray situation. They're expecting you there."

Maria was confused. Why would her father send this person, rather than come himself? But she was a little jet-lagged and had more immediate questions.

"I don't see what's so urgent," Maria said. "I only just got here. I need a shower. And my hair's a mess."

"Your hair's fine," Maria was assured. "You've never looked better. Your father is already talking to the press. He said to tell you that it's important to react quickly. He'll tell you what to say downstairs."

"All right. It was good of you to bring the message. I'm coming." Maria put her shoes back on and checked her make-up. She didn't like it when her father told her what to say. Maria had a mind of her own. As she walked towards the lift she made a decision: this would be her last year on the circuit. With Sue Murray out of the way, Maria could go for the Grand Slam, then, whatever the result, retire as the undisputed world number one. She would marry Oswaldo and have lots of babies. After all, she'd earned plenty of money. Why be greedy? She should enjoy life while she was still young...

"I held the lift for you."

Maria noticed that the door to the lift was propped open by a tennis racket. But the lift itself had gone, leaving a black hole in its wake.

"It doesn't seem to have worked," Maria said, reaching forward to press the call button. Her companion leaned forward too – to remove the racket, Maria thought. But then she felt a hand pressing firmly against her back.

"Hey, wha——?"

Maria was propelled forward, into the lift shaft. She screamed, but her cries went unheard, as the doors closed above her and the tennis star crashed on to the concrete floor, ten flights below.

1

Kelly Christian sat in the hotel lobby, idly flicking through the sports pages of *Le Monde*. She found the tennis tournament preview and was about to apply her schoolgirl French to it. Then a well-groomed young man sat down next to her. He was a year or two older than her – twenty at most: strong jaw, brown eyes and long, curly hair which was the same light-brown shade as Kelly's own.

"You like sport?" he asked in a heavy French accent.

Kelly smiled. "A lot."

"Me too."

The young man smiled back. He had good teeth. Politely, he glanced at the report that she was reading.

"You wish me to translate?"

"Why not? Thank you."

It was unusual for anyone to chat Kelly up on the tour. Most men thought that girls like her were unattainable, or simply too busy. The latter was true – occasionally. But most of the time Kelly was bored. She had no family entourage, only her coach and the occasional hitting partner.

"What does it say?" she asked the young Frenchman, as he skimmed the report. He replied with an expansive, Gallic shrug.

"The dull German is expected to win the Men's. An American woman is making a comeback. Those are the main points. Tennis is so boring these days, don't you think? The men's game – power serves and boring baseline play – hardly any good rallies."

"I'm more interested in the Women's," Kelly admitted.

"But the Women's is so predictable – Hernandez or Murray – good players, sure. Attractive women, too, nice to watch. But they win all the time, and the rest are pygmies."

"I think that's a little unfair," Kelly told him. "There are a lot of young players about to come through. If you went along to Roland Garros, you might see some exciting games."

The Frenchman curled the side of his lips, as if trying to decide whether to take Kelly seriously.

"Perhaps you might persuade me. I could see if there are any tickets left. If, that is, you would accompany me, direct me to the exciting players…"

Kelly raised an eyebrow. She couldn't decide whether to tell her young admirer that she didn't need tickets. But his attention was elsewhere.

"Ah," he said. "Here, I think, is one of the women stars. She was in the final here a few years ago." He was pointing at a tall woman with long, blonde hair who had just swept into the lobby.

"Actually," Kelly told the Frenchman, "Mary's retired. She's my coach."

"Ready?" Mary Porter asked Kelly. "I've got the practice court lined up."

"Ready," said Kelly, standing.

She stood and offered the young man her hand. "Nice to meet you," she said.

"And you. My name is François."

"I'm Kelly … Kelly Christian. And if you're really interested in tennis, I'm playing a qualifier tomorrow. Nothing to stop you coming along. But I can't guarantee that you won't be bored."

"I'll be there," François promised, as Mary swept Kelly away.

Inside the taxi, Mary lectured Kelly.

"Try and keep your mind off boys until you've been knocked out."

"Chance'd be a fine thing," Kelly moaned. "I haven't had a date since finishing at the tennis academy."

9

They turned a corner and found themselves in a traffic jam. "What's going on there?" Kelly asked.

There was a crowd of people outside one of the biggest hotels. Three TV crews blocked the street.

"Isn't that the hotel where Louise is staying?" Kelly asked Mary. Louise Chung was Kelly's closest friend on the tour.

"Yes," Mary told Kelly. "Most of the big players are there. It must be a press conference. I was about to tell you – Sue Murray's pulled out. Injured."

"Pity. I guess that means Hernandez gets to play someone else in the final. What's wrong with Sue?"

Kelly liked Sue Murray. She had spoken to the Australian a couple of times, though she'd never played her. Murray wasn't as stuck-up as Hernandez.

"Shoulder injury," Mary told her. "She was crossing a road when she shouldn't have been and some kid on a motorbike knocked her over. It's obviously serious. They're talking about her taking a year off. It could mean retirement."

"How awful."

"Awful for her, yes. But she's had several good years. It means more opportunity for you. Think positively."

The taxi finally managed to swerve round the last of the TV crews.

"Hold on," Kelly said.

"Arrêtez-vous ici," Mary told the driver. "What is it?" she asked Kelly.

"Over there. Look."

Kelly's friend, Louise Chung, was standing outside the hotel with a young American player, Lacy Cannon. The girls had their arms round each other. Both were sobbing.

"I need to see what's wrong," Kelly insisted.

"Of course."

Mary followed Kelly out of the cab.

"Louise, Lacy, what is it?"

Louise looked up but was too overcome to talk.

"There's been a terrible accident," Lacy told Kelly, her voice cracking with emotion. "We both saw the body. It was horrible."

Kelly put an arm round her Chinese friend.

"Body?" Mary Porter asked. "Who?"

"Maria Hernandez," Lacy told them. "She's dead."

2

The rumours spread from locker-room to locker-room, getting more and more bizarre. Officially, Maria Hernandez died in a freak accident. Her family were supposed to be suing the hotel involved for several billion dollars. Unofficially, she had committed suicide because she had been dumped by her secret lover, a top male star. Or she was under the influence of hallucinogenic drugs and thought she could levitate down the lift shaft. Or she had been murdered by a different lover, a jealous millionaire whose baby she was carrying.

"Every cloud has a silver lining," Mary told Kelly the following morning, as they arrived for practice.

"Like what?"

"With Maria dead and Murray injured, there are two more places in the Open. The committee's given them to you and Elaine Murdoch."

"Really?"

Kelly was elated, and immediately felt guilty for feeling that way. But this would be her first direct entry in a Grand Slam tournament. Kelly was seventeen and had turned professional at the beginning of the year, at the same time as Louise, who was a year older. Elaine Murdoch was a sixteen-year-old white South African, better known for her dazzling blonde looks than for her tennis. Kelly didn't like her.

Making friends was hard on the Women's tennis tour. The temperature was cool. Fights and fallings out were commonplace. Kelly was closest to her coach, Mary.

But Mary was twice her age. Sometimes she acted more like a stern mother than a friend, and Kelly resented her. Mary said that there used to be real camaraderie between players on the tour. Kelly found it hard to believe. There was too much cause for rivalry. Still, she and Louise had become close, even though Louise was in the top fifty, while Kelly was outside the hundred. Maybe Louise being a more successful player made it easier for them to be friends. They didn't think of themselves as being in competition with each other.

It might have seemed more natural for Kelly to be friends with Lacy Cannon. Lacy was the same age as Kelly, and American too, but had become a pro as soon as she turned sixteen. Therefore, it was no surprise that she was ranked a little higher than Kelly. However, in this sport, you were only as good as your last game. Rankings could change dramatically overnight. Lacy had a huge serve, but Kelly thought her own game was better. She resented Lacy's ranking. It didn't help that Lacy's family were rich, while Kelly's weren't. Kelly had to rely on bank loans and help from the American Tennis Association to pay for her coach.

"Let's get on with it," Mary said, the moment they arrived on court. "Today, we'll concentrate on your backhand. Your opponent will exploit any weakness she can find there. I want you to put the balls back as short as you can, forcing me to the net. That way, you'll tire your opponent out."

"Who am I playing?" Kelly asked.

"I'll tell you later."

Mary wanted Kelly to concentrate on technique, not think about the individual player. They pounded balls at each other on the red clay courts, honing the skills which Mary thought needed most attention. Only when they had practised for two hours did Mary tell Kelly who she was to play the next day.

"Zbignew."

Kelly groaned. The statuesque Russian was one of the most powerful players on the circuit. Her serve was stronger than many men's. However, in the last two seasons, Karla Zbignew had slipped out of the top ten.

"She's not as powerful as she was," Mary explained. "And I know her weaknesses inside out. But her serve is still very strong. Much better than mine. We need to find you someone decent to practise against this afternoon. Who was that young British player you worked with at Wimbledon last year?"

"Andrew Kerr."

"You got on well with him, didn't you?"

"I did," Kelly admitted. "But he's not playing. I checked. I guess he couldn't afford to come and try to qualify."

"Shame. We'll have to find you someone else."

For a few days, at the Wimbledon Junior tournament last year, Kelly thought she and Andrew might have something other than tennis going on. They'd gone out, held hands, kissed good night. But, since Wimbledon, she hadn't heard from him.

"Who's that?" Mary asked, pointing at a spectator by the fence.

Kelly recognized her handsome young Frenchman from the hotel – François.

"It's the guy I met yesterday. I'll just say hello."

Kelly waved to François.

"I thought you were playing in a qualifier today," he said.

"They gave me a wild card at the last minute," she told him.

Then she noticed what he was wearing. Expensive whites and tennis shoes. "I didn't know you played."

"Ah," François smiled in a flirtatious way. "I have a confession to make. I'm afraid that, yesterday, I was … teasing you. I knew you were a player."

"And you?"

"I'm in the Junior tournament."

"You look too old."

"I'm eighteen in August."

"What's your serve like?" Kelly asked him.

"Why don't I show you?"

François's serve was formidable: better than Andrew Kerr's. He seemed happy to help Kelly practise for nearly an hour. When they were through, Kelly insisted on buying him lunch in the cafeteria. She wanted to find out more about him, but Mary dominated the conversation. François seemed to be in awe of the former star.

"You don't play any more?" he asked her. "But you're so young."

Mary was dismissive: "I'm thirty-five soon, so I'll qualify as a veteran. Maybe I'll play again then.

Meanwhile, coaching Kelly and doing bits of TV commentary suits me fine."

They talked a little about Maria Hernandez. The police weren't giving out much information and rumours were still rife. Then, after lunch, Kelly practised with François for three more hours, under Mary's close supervision.

"Thank you," Kelly said to François when they were done. She was tired, but he seemed unruffled. "You're really good. Will you turn pro?"

François gave another of his big shrugs.

"Maybe. Maybe not. I want to go to university. The life of a tennis bum doesn't appeal to me. Though, maybe if I was guaranteed to meet up with you…" He finished the sentence with a flirtatious grin. Kelly blushed.

"I'm afraid that the Men's and Women's tours don't meet up very often."

"I know. But we're both here now. What are you doing tonight?" As François smiled seductively at her, Mary interrupted the conversation.

"Kelly isn't allowed out the night before a match. Ask her tomorrow."

When Kelly got back to the hotel she found that Louise had checked in. The slim, wide-eyed girl joined Kelly as she picked at a salad in the hotel restaurant.

"Isn't this a bit down-market for you?" Kelly

asked as Louise sat down. Louise came from a very poor background, much poorer than Kelly's. But she was regarded as a very promising player and already had endorsement contracts with two big Hong Kong companies. She wore their logos and appeared in ads. They paid her enough to afford five-star travel and have homes in Hong Kong and Malibu.

"I couldn't stay in that hotel any more," Louise said emotionally. "Not after what happened to Maria."

"But surely it was an accident?" Kelly said. "You're not superstitious."

Louise made a gesture as though throwing salt over her shoulder.

"My psychologist back in California would say 'if you feel jinxed, then you are jinxed'. There's a bad atmosphere in that hotel. I want to stay well away from it. You know what makes the whole thing worse?"

"What?"

"I should have been playing Maria tomorrow. Instead I face Elaine Murdoch. I've never played Maria. Now I never will. I could have learned a lot from her."

"I'm glad it's Elaine you're playing, not me," Kelly said.

Louise smiled ruefully.

"Me too. Tell me something more cheerful."

So Kelly told her about François. Louise wanted to know everything about him.

"It'll probably come to nothing," Kelly ended. "These things usually do."

"You never know," said Louise. "But now, I must have an early night."

It was nearly nine. Both girls went up to bed. At least Kelly could afford a room to herself in Paris. Usually she shared with Mary. But she'd made it to the third round of the Spanish Open. The prize money was paying for their hotel.

It was lonely, being in a strange, foreign city, on her own. Kelly came from Nahant, Massachusetts, a small town, and her friends there thought that Kelly lived an incredibly exotic life. She wasn't old enough to do the full tour yet – you had to be eighteen for that – but her schedule took in Barcelona, Paris, London. Her friends didn't know how little time Kelly had to see these cities.

Now, instead of sleeping, Kelly found herself worrying: wasn't it a coincidence that the game's two top stars had both had accidents in the same week? Suppose they weren't accidents? Touring tennis players were ferocious gossips, and there were rumours going round of some terrible curse. The question on Kelly's mind would be keeping dozens of other players awake tonight.

Which of us is going to be next?

3

"Isn't it brilliant?" Elaine Murdoch said, sitting next to Kelly in the changing-room. "Our first Grand Slam tournament and we didn't even have to qualify."

Kelly nodded politely. She still felt guilty about Hernandez and Murray. She didn't need reminding about them by the perky South African.

"I'd rather have got it another way," she told Elaine.

"Get it while you can," Elaine said. "You might not get many chances."

Elaine Murdoch was a year younger than Kelly, but she had turned professional at the earliest possible moment, as soon as she turned fifteen. Until the mid-90s, she would have been able to start at thirteen, but then the rules were tightened to protect young players from physical and mental burn-out. Elaine's career began well. She quickly got into the top hundred. With her good looks, and the end of apartheid, she had no trouble getting both endorsement deals and modelling contracts. But this kind of success got in the way of her tennis. Maybe, as some people said, Elaine didn't train hard enough. Whatever the reason, she had yet to gain the success predicted for her. Recently, her ranking had started to slip.

"Good luck," Elaine said, as she went out to warm up.

"Same to you," said Kelly, though both girls knew she wanted Louise to win.

Kelly and Louise exchanged anxious smiles as the Chinese girl followed Elaine out into the stadium. Then Kelly followed Zbignew out. The Russian was two inches taller and two stone heavier than she was. Kelly hoped she could withstand her heavy serve. There was polite applause as they stepped on to the red clay of Roland Garros. Kelly glanced around at the crowd, picking out where Mary was sitting. She was pleased to see François, wearing Aviator sunglasses, sitting directly behind her coach.

Before Kelly knew what was going on, Karla Zbignew's first serve was thundering towards her.

Kelly felt enormous relief when she connected with it. But the ball refused to go back into play. It hurtled towards the spectators in the stadium. Kelly got the next one back, but Zbignew returned with a drop shot which left Kelly stranded at the wrong side of the court. Thirty-love. Then Zbignew aced her again. Kelly returned the next serve, but got caught with a drop shot. She'd been blanked in her first game.

After this humiliation, it got easier. Kelly held her serve. She started getting the odd point on Zbignew's serve, but it was heavy going. At four games all, there was applause from a nearby court. Someone had won already. Next game, Kelly got to deuce before losing. Three games later, they were in a tie-break.

Zbignew looked annoyed. She hadn't expected to have to work this hard. *I've got to press my advantage*, Kelly thought. She won her first serve, and flashed a big smile at Mary and François as they changed ends. Zbignew won her first serve easily, but Kelly emerged from the rally that followed with a point, then won both of her serves. 4-1. Suddenly, Zbignew crumpled. She double faulted, then gave Kelly such an easy serve that it was easy to lob it beyond her reach.

Kelly had six set points, yet still felt like her game could fall apart at any moment. In junior tournaments, at moments like these, she sometimes froze.

Kelly put as much top spin on her serve as she could. Karla Zbignew barely connected with it and the first set was Kelly's. The applause was deafening.

It would have been easy at this point to become excited and overconfident, but Kelly remembered her coach's advice – "treat every point like it's the last one, or it soon will be" – and concentrated even harder. She had Zbignew on the run now. Kelly could return her serve easily and force her to come to the net. Zbignew liked to play from the baseline, while Kelly tried to use the whole court. In the first game of the second set, Kelly nearly broke her, but Karla came back. Kelly evened the score with a love game, her first of the match.

After that, Karla seemed to stop trying. Kelly broke her easily, and the Russian only scored seven points in the remainder of the match. Kelly had won 7-6, 6-1. The second set took less than fifteen minutes. Karla Zbignew shook Kelly's hand and muttered something indecipherable as they came off the court.

Exhilarated, Kelly spotted Louise in the audience. Her friend gave her a thumbs up. She had won too. Kelly suddenly began to take in what had happened. She had made it to the second round of the French Open. After waving at François and Mary, she hurried inside to ring her parents. Never mind the expense.

Kelly bumped into Lacy Cannon in the queue for the phone booths.

"How'd you get on?" Lacy asked.

"Won in straight sets: 7-6, 6-1."

"Brilliant. That'll boost your rating."

"How about you?" Kelly asked Lacy.

"6-2, 6-2. But my opponent was a dog. Local girl who got in on a wild card."

Two phones became free and the girls went to make their calls. Kelly's parents were ecstatic. They'd made big sacrifices so that she could afford to play tennis. They both worked and couldn't afford time off to travel with her.

"But we're with you in spirit," her mother said. "If you make it to the final we'll find a way to come over."

"If I make it to the final I can afford to buy your tickets," Kelly said. "But I'll be lucky to get through the next round."

When the money had run out, Kelly went back to look for Mary and François. Lacy, she noticed, was still talking on the phone.

"Great," she heard her say. "That's terrific news. Thanks again."

"François had to go," Mary told her, "to warm up for a game."

"I should go and watch him," Kelly said.

"Not now. We have lots of things to go over while Zbignew's fresh in your mind. I told François he could come by the hotel for a drink later on."

"Good," Kelly said. "I'll just find Louise. Then I'll join you."

Louise wasn't in the player's lounge. Maybe she'd already gone back to the hotel. From the scoreboard, Kelly saw that her friend had slaughtered Elaine Murdoch: 6-1, 6-0. The South African girl was sitting in a corner, looking fed up. Kelly decided that it would be diplomatic to avoid her. She pretended to look at the TV screen. On Eurosport, Jessie-Ray Connor, former teenage prodigy, was attempting a comeback. As Jessie-Ray took the first set, Kelly quietly sloped out of the lounge to join Mary in a courtesy car to the hotel. She hoped that François was also winning.

Kelly and Mary spent the next hour dissecting the match against Zbignew.

"You did well," Mary told Kelly. "Your backhand is really improving and your serve was the strongest it's ever been. But you gave Karla too much control. She forced most of your errors. You were out of position way too often, while nearly all of her mistakes were unforced. She was expecting an easy game and she got rattled. You can't rely on that happening next round."

Kelly knew what her coach meant: tennis was only partly about skill. Psychology and tactics were equally important. Most of the time, you didn't win a game: your opponent lost it. That was what had happened today.

When they were done, Kelly tried to find Louise again. No one was answering the phone in her room, so Kelly went down to the bar. If François turned up early, he'd find her there. As Kelly walked through the lobby, looking out for her Chinese friend, she nearly bumped into a tall man with dark, receding hair and a light jacket. He looked vaguely familiar. Kelly muttered an apology.

"Not at all. My fault."

The man gave Kelly a deep, piercing stare. Hurriedly, she brushed past him, into the hotel bar. Louise was sitting with her Japanese coach, Tetsuo. She greeted Kelly loudly.

"Well done! I heard that you were superb this afternoon."

"I played OK," Kelly said. "Congratulations on your win."

"A walk-over," Louise told her. "Elaine's on the skids."

Tetsuo ordered Kelly a *café au lait*. As the two girls discussed their games, a shadow crossed Louise's face.

"Uh-oh," she said.

"What's wrong?" Kelly asked.

"Just someone I'd rather not see."

Kelly glanced round. The sinister man with the dark hair and linen jacket was standing by the bar. He raised a glass at the two girls. Kelly turned back.

She was surprised to see Louise returning the greeting with a forced smile.

"Who's that?" she asked her friend.

"Peter Kong. You must have heard of him."

Kelly had. The Californian millionaire was a talking-point amongst the girls on the tour, but she had never seen him before. Kong was an orphan millionaire. His parents owned a vast motel chain in the USA. Both died in a car crash when he was thirty, five years ago. Since then, Peter Kong had spent their money following the women's tennis circuit. Kong lavished gifts on female stars he admired. He was said to have bought Maria Hernandez a Lotus Elan and paid for a heated swimming-pool to be installed in her Malibu home.

"What does Kong want with you?" Kelly asked Louise.

Her friend shrugged.

"Tetsuo says I have to be nice to him. He has connections which helped me get my first endorsement contract. And – you know how it is – he paid for a couple of air flights. When my mum was sick last year, he had his private jet take me home to visit her."

"I didn't know."

Louise had kept very quiet about this relationship, Kelly thought.

"I'd better go and have a word with him," Louise added. "Excuse me."

"Sure."

Louise walked up to the bar. Kong kissed her on the cheek. He was creepy, Kelly decided. But she couldn't blame Louise for accepting his largesse. Louise's parents were peasants. They had little money until recently, when Louise bought them a flat in Hong Kong. Kelly couldn't understand, though, why Maria Hernandez, with all her money, took gifts from Kong. Now that Maria was dead, would Louise be number one in the millionaire's affections? It wasn't a prospect which Kelly would relish.

"Hey!"

Kelly looked up. It was François. She was relieved to see his smiling face.

"How did you get on?" she asked.

"Won. 6-2, 6-2."

"I'm sorry I didn't see you play."

"I'm nothing special," he insisted. "You were great today."

"Zbignew tanked in the second set."

François shook his head.

"She only gave up because she saw that she couldn't beat you."

"Maybe…" Kelly said. "But I wouldn't have played so well if I hadn't had you as a hitting partner."

The waiter came to their table with two glasses of champagne.

"What's this?" François asked. "Are you … what's the word … *psychic*? Did you know that I'd won and would come straight here?"

"Not me," Kelly said, turning round. "Him."

Louise and Kong raised their glasses to François and Kelly.

"Congratulations," Kong called out. "All three of you winners."

François smiled. "Thanks very much."

Then he resumed his conversation with Kelly. François probably thought that Kong was Louise's boyfriend, although he was twice her age. In tennis, lots of girls had much older boyfriends – their trainers, mainly – though they kept quiet about these relationships in public. How did Kong know that François had won, Kelly wondered. He was standing too far away to have overheard their conversation. Anyway, why would Kong be interested in some French lad playing in the Juniors? Kelly thought about the way he had looked at her earlier and wondered whether—

"Hey, are you listening?" François complained.

"I'm sorry, I was miles away."

"Perhaps you were wondering about who you'll be playing in the next round?"

"It had crossed my mind, yes."

"They were just putting the notice up when I left the stadium."

"Really?"

François took another sip of his champagne.

"Come on," Kelly said. "Who?"

"Another young American – the one they call the *cannonball*."

"Lacy."

"Yes. She should be easier than Zbignew, no?"

Kelly would rather not be playing Lacy.

"I don't know," she replied. "Maybe. She's beaten me a couple of times, but I think I've improved a lot since then. Of course, she's improved too. Her serve's incredible, and she's an intelligent player – a lot like Hernandez. It's not an easy draw."

Then Kelly thought about Maria Hernandez.

"I haven't seen today's papers," she said. "What are they saying about her death?"

François leant over and lightly pressed her hand.

"Don't think about that now," he said. "Think about winning. You know, there are girls who would kill to be in the position you're in."

Kelly flinched at François's choice of words, but he was right. She smiled coquettishly and squeezed his hand back. For a tender moment, she was wildly happy, and the world seemed full of promise.

When the moment passed, they were both standing to leave. François leant towards Kelly. She thought he was going to kiss her. He did, but on the forehead. Kelly glanced over at Louise. Instead she saw the sinister Peter Kong, staring at her.

4

It was the night before Kelly's second-round match against Lacy Cannon. All day, Kelly had practised with Mary and François. She was growing more and more attracted to the young Frenchman. He wasn't pushy or pretentious. Most of the men you met on the tour looked down on you one way or the other. They wanted to use you. To François, tennis was just a game. He had his priorities right. He was interested in Kelly as a person, not as a player. Last night he had taken her to a movie. It was American, but dubbed into French, so he had to keep whispering into her ear to explain what was going on. Afterwards, he took her back to the hotel, and they kissed properly for the first time: only a light peck on the lips, but it was a move in the right direction.

Tonight, though, she wouldn't see him. Kelly showered after practice and walked through the players' lounge, looking for Mary. Instead, she nearly bumped into her next day's opponent. But Lacy was too distracted to notice Kelly. She'd seen Elaine Murdoch first.

"Hi, Elaine. How're you doing?" Lacy said.

The young South African girl had been practising all day but still looked glamorous. *I could take some lessons in styling from her,* Kelly thought.

"Not great," Elaine said. "Got knocked out of the doubles this afternoon. I'm off to England tonight, start my grass practice for Wimbledon early."

"See you there," Lacy said.

Kelly didn't relish seeing Lacy the evening before their match. She was just about to slip past both the girls when she overheard Elaine saying, "What's that on your skirt?"

Lacy pulled the skirt out of her bag, looking bashful.

"They haven't done a brilliant job of sewing it on, have they? It's a Lacoste crocodile emblem. I got the endorsement contract yesterday."

"How could you?" Elaine's voice turned to a snarl. Kelly paused at the door and looked round. "You must have known that my contract with Lacoste was up for renewal. What did you do?" Elaine asked. "Ring them straight after the match yesterday and say I'm doing better than Elaine

Murdoch and I'm better looking than her, too, so give me a contract?"

Lacy became uneasy.

"Elaine, you've got it all wrong. This has nothing to do with me. It was the agency."

"I thought we were friends," Elaine whinged.

"We are," Lacy protested. "Look, Elaine, it's not a big deal."

"It might not be a big deal to you," Elaine went on, "but it is to me. I needed that money. And to lose it to an overweight, underskilled—"

"I'm not taking any more of this." Lacy began to walk off. She was very pretty, and photographed well, but she was sensitive about her weight, which went up and down. Elaine grabbed her shoulder.

"I haven't finished with you yet."

"Look," Lacy asserted, "I didn't even know you had a contract with Lacoste."

"Pull the other one."

"And my agent's been negotiating with them for weeks. The fact that it happened yesterday was only a coincidence."

"Sure, and the phone call I got this morning saying that they weren't renewing – that was a coincidence too, was it? You're unbelievable!"

Elaine leant forward and snatched the skirt from Lacy's bag. She began to tear the symbol from it.

"Leave that alone!"

Lacy tried to grab the skirt back. The next thing

Kelly knew, fists were flying. She looked round. The lounge was deserted. Kelly was the only one who could stop them before they really hurt each other.

"Break it up!"

Kelly pushed her way between them, hoping that she wouldn't get hit herself.

"There are some press just round the corner," she lied. "Do you want to get in the papers?"

This approach worked. Elaine scowled and stalked off out of the lounge. Lacy picked up her torn skirt, put it in her bag and thanked Kelly.

"I don't know what came over her. If you hadn't…"

"No problem," Kelly said. "See you tomorrow."

Kelly thought about what had happened as she travelled back to the hotel. Lacy was ambitious. Anyone could see that. She'd known perfectly well that she was taking that contract from Elaine. But, as Mary kept telling Kelly, there was no room for sentiment in professional tennis. Elaine was in direct competition with Lacy, off the court as well as on. With Lacy on the way up and Elaine on the way down, it would be hard for them to stay friends. Maria Hernandez's death would mean that there were more endorsement contracts up for grabs, too. Both girls would want them.

Kelly would have liked an endorsement contract

or two herself. She needed the money badly. It was time, Kelly decided, for her to jazz up her image, the way Lacy had: a new hair-do, a sexier outfit. She would discuss it with Mary tomorrow. Kelly hated all the paraphernalia which went with tennis these days. But careers in women's tennis could be very short. One injury, like the one Sue Murray sustained recently, and you could be out for good. You had to go for the money.

Kelly slept badly, as she always did the night before important games. She woke at five and couldn't get back to sleep again. She did warm-up exercises and tried to read. Finally, she went for a walk. There was a news-stand opening up and she looked for a recent American paper. The only ones they had were two days old. She was about to buy the *International Herald Tribune* when she spotted the latest issue of the *National Enquirer*. The headline made her blood run cold.

"EXCLUSIVE! MARIA HERNANDEZ WAS MURDERED!"

The bullet-line beneath read: "Death stalks the stars". A quick glance inside the paper showed that there was no evidence to back the story up, only speculation. "Did she jump or was she pushed?" the article asked. "Sexy star had no reason to kill herself." But the *Enquirer* couldn't come up with a single person who had a grudge against Hernandez, only suggestions of an anonymous "rejected lover".

Kelly walked off without buying anything.

The match against Lacy was an anti-climax. After three-all, Lacy's game crumpled, and she lost the next six games. Half-way through the second set, Lacy managed a small revival, breaking Kelly once, but still lost 6-2. The match lasted barely an hour. They shook hands and went inside to mild applause.

"You played well," Lacy told Kelly.

"Thanks."

"You know, I reckon we could learn from each other. If you ever need a doubles partner..."

"I'm kind of committed to Louise," Kelly said, then added, "But thanks again. I hope the row with Elaine didn't affect your game."

Lacy gave a little shrug, as though to say that of course the fight had spoiled her game but she was far too diplomatic to say it aloud. Instead, she said:

"Thanks for getting between me and Elaine the way you did. It could have been a lot worse."

"No problem."

Then Lacy was joined by her parents, who had travelled over to see the game. From the look on their faces, it was clear they'd expected her to win easily. Kelly rang home, then was in time to watch the final set of Louise's match.

* * *

Officially, Louise's opponent was the number four seed but, with Murray and Hernandez gone, she was really number two. Petra Gordon had won the first set 6-4, but Louise came back to take the second by the same margin. Louise was playing the best Kelly had ever seen her. Kelly was glad that she couldn't play Louise before the final because, on this form, she would get slaughtered. Louise took the third set 6-3. The crowd applauded warmly, but there weren't many of them there. Most people were on the adjoining court, where the American Jessie-Ray Connor had beaten the number three seed in straight sets, 6-4, 6-0. Her comeback was in full swing.

"It looks like you'll be meeting her in the final," Kelly told Louise after the game.

"We'll see," Louise said, as they walked back into their hotel. "There are three more rounds between here and there."

"Most of the seeds are already gone. On your form, you could beat anyone." Louise shrugged. Kelly pressed the call button for the elevator. Suddenly, a journalist ran up to them and poked a cassette recorder into Kelly's face.

"You've got the wrong person," Kelly said. "Louise just beat a top seed."

"It's the next round I'm interested in," the journalist said, getting into the lift with them. "How do you feel about playing Jessie-Ray Connor?"

"I didn't know I was," Kelly said. "I try to take it one match at a time."

"Please," the journalist begged in an English accent, "give me something." Kelly thought. The lift slowed down, and halted.

"Jessie-Ray was a hero to me when I was younger," Kelly said. "I really hope that her comeback is successful. It wouldn't be fair if she was remembered for the scandals in her life rather than her superb tennis. I'm more than happy just to have got to the third round here. That said, I'll give it my best shot."

"Can you win?" the journalist asked.

They still weren't moving. Louise pressed the lift button in agitation.

"On any given day, anyone can win," Kelly said. "Even little ol' me."

The journalist turned the tape recorder off.

"Thanks," she said to Kelly. Then she turned to Louise. "What's wrong with the lift?"

"I don't—"

Before Louise could finish her sentence, the lift lurched to one side. Kelly grabbed her friend's arm but it was the journalist who looked terrified.

"I knew I shouldn't have got in here with two tennis players," she said, pressing the emergency button. "Everyone knows there's a psycho on the loose."

"Don't get hysterical," Louise said. "What happened to Maria was an accident."

"Oh, sure," said the journalist, as the lift lurched again. "And what happened to Sue Murray the day before was an accident too, was it? The motorcyclist who drove straight at her. She was nearly killed. The top two women players disposed of in two days. Quite a coincidence." As she spoke, her voice had risen and risen, until it became a high-pitched squeak.

"Where did you hear that the motorcyclist hit her deliberately?" Kelly asked.

"The police won't definitely confirm it, but the press all know. There's something fishy about Hernandez's death as well. Accident or suicide, there was no way she could have gone down that shaft unless the lift doors were propped open. And there was nothing which could be used as a prop left behind."

Nervously, the reporter's fingers jabbed the emergency button again and again.

"How high up are we?" she asked the two tennis players. "Would we survive the fall?"

"Sure," Kelly said cynically. "Whoever it is only wants to injure us. They'll be happy to put us on crutches. Nothing for you to worry about."

The lift shuddered again. All three women trembled. Then it continued its journey to the fourth floor, arriving safely, as though nothing had happened.

5

Jessie-Ray Connor was a living legend. She was born Jessie Jones, daughter of a dentist and a pro-basketball player. Jessie first picked up a racket when she was three years old. She turned professional the week before her fourteenth birthday. In the next two years Jessie won numerous tournaments, including three out of the four Grand Slam tournaments. She was a clean cut, all-American superstar. She was beautiful, too, endlessly pursued by boys and men.

Then it all began to go wrong. After a tip-off, police found cannabis in her hotel room while she was playing at the US Open. Jessie claimed it was planted on her and got away with a misdemeanour charge. The Japanese weren't so lenient when cocaine was found in her kit bag at a Tokyo tournament. Jessie said that she'd been set up again, but was thrown out of the tournament and deported.

Jessie's sponsors queued up to drop her. A convenient injury took her out of the game for a few months. The next time she was on the front pages, it wasn't for winning a tennis tournament, but for dating a well-known Australian rock singer. She left home after a well-publicized row with her parents and moved in with a boxer, Tim Connor. Overweight and unfit, she tried to return to tennis, but was knocked out after the first round of three consecutive tournaments. During her final press conference, she explained why: she was pregnant.

At the age when Kelly was beginning her professional career, Jessie retired from hers. She married the father of her baby and began using her middle name. She let her looks grow shabby, so that people wouldn't recognize her in the street. For a year, the now Jessie-Ray Connor managed to find the obscurity she craved. Tim retired from the ring. At first, he lived off her money. Later, he was arrested and given a five-year sentence for handling stolen property.

When Jessie-Ray next appeared in the news, two years later, she was in court again. The former star was divorcing her imprisoned husband, who wanted half of the millions she had earned from tennis. At the same time, Jessie-Ray's parents were seeking to deny their daughter access to the trust fund set up during her tennis career. She was meant to get the money when she was twenty-one. Her parents said Jessie-Ray would spend the millions she'd earned on her drug habit.

Eventually, a compromise was reached. The husband was paid off with an undisclosed sum. Jessie-Ray was given a substantial income from the trust fund, but most of her money was set aside in order to provide secure provision for her son, Nathan. Once more, she returned to obscurity. Most people thought that this was the last they would hear from Jessie-Ray Connor.

But they were wrong. A few days before the French Open, Jessie-Ray, now twenty-two, called a press conference to announce that she had spent the last nine months preparing for a comeback. She'd been granted a wild card, allowing her entry to the French Open, which was the first of the three Grand Slam tournaments she'd won eight years before.

That night, Kelly and Mary watched a video of Jessie-Ray's first round performance. She'd not got an easy draw. Her opponent was Rosie Velasquez, from Spain, the number twelve seed. Jessie-Ray looked healthy and fit, but Velasquez took the first game easily. She didn't win another. Jessie-Ray had a dazzling range of shots, and commanded the court like she'd never been away. As Kelly watched, she wasn't sure whether to be impressed or depressed. It reminded her of when she was nine years old, watching Jessie Jones winning the US Open.

Mary changed tapes and they watched Jessie-Ray's victory in the next round. Her play was even more impressive.

"I hope you're not trying to tell me that was a flash in the pan," Kelly said to Mary.

Her coach shook her head. "It was a stunning performance. But she's not as good as she used to be … yet."

Kelly put her head in her hands. Mary came over and spoke gently to her.

"I want to tell you something I haven't told you before."

Dutifully, Kelly listened. Mary's face became serious.

"You know when I decided to give up being a pro? It was Wimbledon, six years ago. I was still the number one seed when I met Jessie-Ray in the semi. She was sixteen. I'd played her four times before and we were even. I'd won the more important games, though, and she wasn't good on grass. I thought I was set up for a final. I was wrong. That day, I was humiliated. I went out 6-2, 6-2. Jessie lost to Sue Murray in the final. But you should understand … Jessie Jones was a better player than

43

Murray, or Hernandez, or me. She could have been the best ever. I knew that I'd never be able to play as well as she could."

Mary sighed.

"I kept playing for a few months, but the spark had gone. So, on my thirtieth birthday, I retired. A short while later, Jessie self destructed. You know, I could have played on for another two or three years. It's funny the way things work out."

Mary went quiet, lost in thought.

"Is this meant to make me feel better about losing to her the day after tomorrow?" Kelly asked.

Mary laughed.

"Not at all. I haven't finished my story yet. The first three years of retirement were hard for me. Learning the skills to be a commentator didn't come naturally, and I couldn't find any young players who I really wanted to coach. Then someone from the American Tennis Association told me about you. They told me about your background, that you wouldn't be able to afford to pay my expenses at first, but that I should see you play before I turned you down.

"That day, watching you play at the Academy, I saw someone who had the potential to be as good as Jessie, or better. That's why I took you on. I only wanted to coach a player who had the potential to be better than I was."

Kelly was taken aback. This was the first time

that they'd really discussed Mary's reasons for being her coach.

"But I'm already older than Jessie was when she stopped playing," Kelly protested, "and I'm nowhere near as good as she was."

Mary shook her head. "People progress at different rates. It's not always good to start as early as Jessie did. Look at Elaine Murdoch, constantly plagued by small injuries and unable to improve her game on what it was a year ago. No, the important thing is that you're improving all the time. And Jessie isn't as good as she was. Probably, she never will be. The game's changed in the five years since she left. You've got a chance against her. But only if you believe in yourself. And whatever happens on that court, you'll learn a lot. It's a great opportunity. You must give it your best shot."

Mary rewound the video.

"I think I've spotted some weaknesses. Here's the first of the things that I wanted to show you."

Later, François came to Kelly's room for the first time. They sat close together on the bed. Kelly figured that, tonight, something was going to happen between them. She didn't want to talk about taking François to Wimbledon. It would jinx the evening if, for whatever reason, he couldn't go. They talked about their families for a while. When they were relaxed enough to get more intimate, they kissed. Then there was a knock on the door.

"It's only eight," François protested.

"That's not Mary's knock," Kelly told him.

It was Louise. Kelly's friend was upset.

"I'm sorry to interrupt," she said. "I've just spent an hour with the police. Can you believe that?"

"Why?" Kelly asked. "What about?"

"Maria's death. They said that they've interviewed everybody who was staying in the hotel but they've only just got around to me because I changed hotels. They made it seem like I was a suspect because I moved here!"

"Calm down," Kelly told her friend. "I'm sure it was just routine."

"I don't know," Louise said. "They kept going on about suspicious circumstances and – you know – English isn't my first language and it isn't theirs either. I'm worried that I might have made myself a suspect."

Kelly didn't know what to say.

"I'm sure you're overreacting," François told Louise. "Everyone knows how stressful the Women's tour is. Hernandez cracked up and killed herself. It could have happened to anyone."

The two girls looked at François. He seemed to realize that his comments weren't terribly tactful.

"Maybe I should go," he said.

Kelly wanted to hold him, to kiss him, but loyalty to her friend had to come first.

"I'll see you tomorrow," she said.

"Of course."

He gave her a small hug. Then, with the open door blocking them from Louise, they had a long kiss. Kelly let her eyes say what she was feeling, hoping that he felt the same way. Then he was gone.

"I'm sorry I interrupted you," Louise said. "If I'd known…"

"No. It's OK, really. He couldn't stay long anyway. Not the night before a match. I had to get a special dispensation from Mary for him to come at all."

They sat down.

"You don't think that Maria was murdered, do you?" Louise asked.

"No," said Kelly. "I'm sure that François was right. Probably, Maria had private problems which none of us knew anything about. But she was world-famous. The police have to investigate thoroughly."

"Suppose she *was* murdered," Louise suggested. "After all, her death leaves the women's game wide open. Plenty of people must be happy to see her gone."

"And most of them have already left Paris after losing in the first two rounds," Kelly said. "So the police can't talk to them any more. That's why they got round to you. But the idea doesn't make sense to me. Can you think of a single girl on the tour who's capable of murder?"

"I guess not," Louise said.

But there was a shadow of a doubt in her voice.

"Have an early night," Kelly said. "You can't let this affect your game."

They talked a little more about their opponents. Louise had what looked like an easy draw, but you could never be sure. Kelly had already written off her chances for the next day, though she pretended optimism. At nine, when she went to bed, her thoughts were filled with François, not Jessie-Ray. For once, on the night before a big match, she slept well, not even stirring when Mary looked in to check that she was sleeping alone.

6

"**Y**our biggest problem is if you freeze up," Mary warned just before Kelly went out on court. "Follow the plan, don't let her fluster you, and you've got a good chance. Remember that."

"Jeu, Madame Connor."

It was 4–3. So far every game had gone with serve, which was unusual in a women's match. Kelly had done what Mary said, trying to stop Jessie-Ray playing her natural game. But Jessie-Ray wasn't letting her play either. The few rallies they had were short. Kelly wanted to come into the net more, to volley, but didn't dare risk it.

"Fault!"

Concentrate! Kelly told herself, as she launched a safe second serve to the left of Jessie-Ray. Her opponent hurried forward and played a backhand volley which caused Kelly to go full stretch for it. She got it back, but had no time to recover. It was easy for Jessie-Ray to lob her, taking the point.

"Zéro–quinze."

Kelly put as much topspin as she could on her first serve. These had been giving Jessie-Ray trouble all day, and she didn't get near this one.

"Fault!"

"Not again!" Kelly said out loud, but she knew better than to complain. She wasn't going to give Jessie-Ray another easy second serve, so she put as much power into her next serve as she had. Third time lucky, she hoped. It went out.

"Zéro–trente."

You're thinking too much, Kelly told herself. *Just play your game. You can beat this woman.* Her next serve aced Jessie-Ray, and the crowd applauded loudly. One more like that and she would be even. As Jessie-Ray reached for the service, Kelly came to the net, hoping to be able to smash a winner off Jessie-Ray's return. But she'd been over confident. The former champion hit a superb passing shot, giving her two break points. Kelly tried to concentrate but, within moments, she had double-faulted again, and Jessie-Ray was serving for the set.

Buoyed by breaking Kelly, Jessie-Ray played superbly. Kelly didn't get a point. As the set ended, she felt the whole match slipping away from her.

At least I got four games against Jessie-Ray, she thought. *I didn't do too badly.*

Kelly felt dowdy, plain. Jessie-Ray looked like an Amazon. She wore a bandanna decorated with the stars and stripes. She played like an Amazon, too. Her serve was stronger than Zbignew's and she frequently sliced it wide into the corner of the court. If Kelly was to return it, she had to anticipate the ball and move fast, catching the ball as soon as it bounced, before it cut unpredictably away. As the second set went on, Kelly found more cracks in Jessie-Ray's armour. She failed to reach a lob and swore. *She can't be all that fit*, Kelly thought, *she's been out of the game too long. If I can take her to a third set, I'll beat her.*

The crowd cheered and cheered as the rallies grew longer. With Jessie-Ray serving at 4-3 down, Kelly got her first break point of the match, 30-40. She scooped up her opponent's serve and returned it to the far corner of the court. Jessie-Ray dived for it, but had no chance. The crowd went wild.

"Egalité."

"What?"

Kelly couldn't conceal her disbelief. Surely the ball hadn't gone out?

"Egalité."

The ball had clearly been in and the crowd were now on Kelly's side. The umpire, however, wasn't going to overrule and Jessie-Ray wasn't making any comment. Kelly had to let it go. But she wasn't going to let the game go. She came in early on the next serve and managed to smash it back over the net.

"Avantage, Mademoiselle Christian."

The next point was the longest rally of the game, but Kelly won it. Now, she was serving to equal the match at one set all. This time, all of her first serves went in and the rallies were shorter. Jessie-Ray gave it everything she had, but still only got one point. After seventy-five minutes of play, Kelly had reversed the score of the first set. They were even at one set all. Kelly was on fire now. She had felt pumped before, but never like this. She could do no wrong.

As Jessie-Ray served to open the next set, Kelly went for everything. She could see that her opponent was flustered. Jessie-Ray was trying to slow the game down, but Kelly wouldn't let her. *If it goes to a third set, try to wear her out*, Mary had counselled. Kelly would make Jessie-Ray feel like she was playing in the eye of a hurricane.

"Egalité."

Kelly was concentrating so hard that she hardly noticed the drops of rain which were beginning to fall on her bare arms. Jessie-Ray's next serve was a demon. Kelly couldn't return it. But she won the next point and the next one.

"Avantage, Mademoiselle Christian."

If she could break Jessie-Ray now, in the first game, then hold her serve, the older American would never come back. *Don't think ahead*, Kelly reminded herself. *Take every point as it comes.* She was enjoying herself more than she ever had done on a court. She felt like her game had finally come together. She couldn't wait for Jessie-Ray to serve the next ball. Yet, instead of serving, Jessie-Ray was talking to the umpire. A drop of cool rain landed on Kelly's fevered brow.

"Le match est suspendu."

There was a groan from the spectators. *Surely*, Kelly thought, *the rain isn't serious enough to stop us in the middle of a game?* But Jessie-Ray was already leaving the court, and the rain was getting heavier. Kelly went inside to the crowd's cheers.

In the locker-room, the two women ignored each other. Kelly had never been in this situation before, but figured that conversation was bound to damage either woman's concentration. She walked through to the refreshment area where Mary was waiting for her.

"You've played brilliantly," her coach assured her. "Apart from the last two games in the first set, I've never seen you better. I want you to move around, keep warmed up. Don't lose any of that energy when you're back out there."

Kelly did as she was told. In the locker-room, she noticed Jessie-Ray brushing her coach away. The former champion sat in a corner, shoulders hunched, a towel wrapped round her. She could have been meditating.

The rain continued. Kelly began to worry. Jessie-Ray was getting time to recover. That wasn't good. Kelly felt sticky and her muscles were beginning to tighten. She needed a shower. But suppose they were ready to start again before she was? Kelly looked outside. The rain was slight, but steady. Then she looked at herself in the mirror. This match was being shown in a hundred countries. If she got one endorsement contract out of it, she might be able to afford better hotels, fly her parents over for Wimbledon. She had to look her best.

She showered quickly, letting the pounding hot water massage her body just long enough to bring everything back to life. Then she dried off and brushed her hair before getting into her spare outfit. She dabbed a little face powder beneath her eyes, where the tension was starting to show. Kelly was lacing up her shoes when she heard Jessie-Ray walking up behind her.

"Time for the show to go on."

Perfect timing, Kelly thought. She walked out on to the number one court, feeling like a million dollars. Jessie-Ray hadn't changed. Her shirt hung lankly off her back and her hair was pushed right back with the bandanna. *She looks like some kind of tribal warrior*, Kelly thought. Then the first serve thundered into play and Kelly waited for the magic to come back.

But the magic had gone. She failed to return Jessie-Ray's serve and, before she knew it, the next two points were gone. When Kelly served, it was as though the second set had never happened. Jessie-Ray went for everything while Kelly tried, hopelessly, to keep up with her. She was broken. Two games later, she was broken again. Two games later, it was all over. Jessie-Ray had blanked her and made it to the quarter-finals.

"You're one hell of a player," Jessie-Ray said as she shook Kelly's hand.

"So are you," Kelly replied.

Yet, in her heart of hearts, she knew that Jessie-Ray hadn't won this match. She, Kelly, had lost it. It was no good blaming the rain.

"Like I said," Mary told Kelly as she left the court. "Even if you don't win, you'll learn a lot."

Yes, thought Kelly. *I've learnt to care more about my game than my hair*. But she didn't say this.

"Where's François?" she asked.

"I've no idea," Mary told her. "He left as soon as the match ended."

This was the last straw. Kelly collapsed into the corner of the locker-room. François didn't come. How could he desert her at a time like this? When Kelly got to her press conference, half an hour late, it was obvious that she'd been crying. But everyone assumed it was for the obvious reason. The journalists were nice to her. None of them asked about her love life — which was a good thing, because it seemed that she no longer had one.

Vanity, Kelly thought. She'd been so keen on looking good, for the press and for François, that she'd lost the game. But how could it be that she'd lost François too? He'd left no message at the hotel and she had no way of contacting him. Kelly had been so confident of his interest in her that she hadn't bothered to get an address or phone number. She didn't even know his second name.

Kelly went through the Juniors' results in *Le Monde*. There were three male players with the initial "F". That hardly helped her to find him. Anyway, if she got the right name, what was she supposed to do? Ring every family with that surname in France and ask them if they had a seventeen-year-old son who played tennis? That would be awkward enough even if she spoke French, which she didn't.

At dinner, she discussed François with Mary, her surrogate mother.

"Some boys are like that," Mary said. "They latch on to a girl while she's being successful, then move on when her star fades."

"I can't believe that François is like that."

"You never do, till afterwards. When I retired from the tour, the kind of men I'd been dating before stopped calling. And I had some major letdowns before that, believe me."

Later, Kelly discussed the situation with Louise. Her friend had never had a boyfriend, but was even more cynical.

"Most of the stories you hear from the other girls are worse," she told Kelly. "They all say that tennis players are fickle users: here today, gone tomorrow."

"Not all of them, surely," Kelly protested.

Louise shrugged.

"That's one reason so many girls have relationships with their coaches or hitting partners. If you're paying the man, he doesn't find it so easy to walk out on you."

Kelly gave up looking for reasons. She tried to make a joke of it.

"Are you trying to tell me something about you and Tetsuo?"

Louise laughed. Her coach was at least forty-five.

"If you believe all the gossip," she said, "there are stranger pairs."

The question remained: what to do now? There were three weeks before Wimbledon. By getting to the third round in France and Spain, Kelly would have lifted her ranking. She wouldn't need to qualify for Wimbledon. But she needed practice.

"There are two tournaments you could play," Mary told Kelly over dinner. "There's the DFS Classic in Edgbaston. That starts tomorrow. We'd have trouble making it. Then there's Eastbourne, which starts the Monday before Wimbledon. Most of the big players will be there."

"What do you suggest?"

"You could do both, but you deserve a break."

"I'd like to stick around in Paris to see how Louise gets on," Kelly said.

"That suits me," Mary told her. "I'm doing some commentary for NBC. They'll pick up my hotel bill but…"

"It's OK," Kelly told her. "I'll share Louise's room."

Kelly dreamt of bumping into François but, of course, she didn't. What would he be doing in the tourist parts of town? He might still be playing in the Juniors but, if so, she didn't want to go. Louise was happy for Kelly to share her hotel room. The two girls read the stories about themselves in the international press. The Maria Hernandez inquest had recorded an open verdict. No one knew what had really happened. The player was buried in the village where she was born. Now the media were anxious to establish a new set of tennis superstars. Louise fitted the bill. She was getting interest from companies wanting her to endorse their products.

Kelly was also getting some interest from sponsors. All of the papers praised the way she had played in the second set against Connor: "True championship potential" said the London *Observer*. But most of the coverage went to Jessie-Ray. "She's back, and she's better than ever!" screamed *The New York Post*. Other papers had more sober assessments. But they agreed that, if Jessie-Ray carried on playing the way she'd started, she might one day gain the world number one slot vacated by Hernandez and Murray.

Both Louise and Jessie-Ray won their quarter-finals. In the semis, Louise lost the opening set against the German number seven, but came back to win the second on a tie-break and demolished her opponent in the third. Jessie-Ray had an easier match. Only Kelly had taken her to a third set. At the final, Kelly sat with Tetsuo and Louise's parents, who had flown over from Hong Kong.

The match was close, and very exciting. After seventy minutes, the players were at one set all. It was very hot out on the red clay courts. Both women were beginning to wilt a little. In the first game of the third set, Jessie-Ray found some extra energy from somewhere. At 3-0, it looked like the American's comeback was complete. But then Louise held her serve and broke back. 3-2. Jessie-Ray broke back. 4-2. This time, Louise broke her and held her serve. They were even. Both women were playing superb tennis, but both were making errors, too. They were tired. Next to her, Louise's father was yelling "Concentrate! Concentrate!" in English. Her mother was shouting something in Chinese. Kelly called out.

"Slow it down! Play your normal game."

You weren't meant to coach from the players' box, but Kelly wasn't Louise's coach. Tetsuo remained silent. Anyway, the advice could have been for either woman. If so, Louise was the one listening. She took her time between points and, as Jessie-Ray charged around the court, Louise conserved her energy for the points that were winnable. Slowly, the balance of the game began to change.

They got to 6-6. There was no tie-break in the final set and Jessie-Ray was showing signs of tiredness. She held her serve to go 7-6, but then Louise held hers and broke in the next game. At

8-7, she was serving for the match. Jessie-Ray got every serve back, and contested every point, but won only one. As Louise got to forty-fifteen the American star threw her racket on to the clay court and let out a huge, exasperated yell.

Jessie-Ray was offered a new racket, but played out the last point with the damaged old one. It didn't matter: she failed to connect with the serve. The French Open had a new, eighteen-year-old champion. In the players' box, Kelly and Louise's parents hugged. On court, Louise lifted the trophy high.

Louise had to do interviews afterwards. Kelly waited for her in the players' lounge, watching TV. Louise gushed for a couple of minutes about how her dream had come true, then went off to talk to the US networks. The presenter asked Mary for a comment.

"Louise has loads of talent," Mary said. "Everybody knows that. Today she showed that she has a champion's temperament, too. In future, she could well be the one player who all the others know is the hardest to beat."

"We're expecting Jessie-Ray any moment. How do you think she did?"

"Pretty good," Mary conceded.

"You and her were great rivals at one point, weren't you?"

"Not really. We only played each other, I think, five times."

"But there was no love lost between you?" The presenter pressed the point.

"Water under the bridge," Mary said.

"Is she as good as she once was?"

"Not yet, no. She's different. She may yet prove to have new strengths."

"The dream nearly came true," Jessie-Ray told the presenter a moment later. "But it turned out to be Louise's day. I'll have other days."

"What's your ambition now?"

"I want to go to Wimbledon. It's the only Grand Slam tournament I never won as a kid. It would mean more to me than anything if I could take it this year."

"Good luck," the presenter said. "It's great to have you back."

"Thanks," said Jessie-Ray. "I'll need all the luck I can get."

Mary was still in the studio, but the two women hadn't spoken to each other. The camera lingered for a moment on the frozen smiles on the faces of the two former stars. Jessie-Ray's smile started to slip and Kelly thought she saw a hard, bitter look, one which showed a different side to Jessie-Ray's personality. Then the picture cut to motor racing.

2

EASTBOURNE

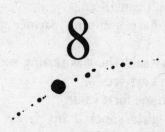

8

For a week each summer, Eastbourne turned into a tennis town. The rest of the time, the large coastal town served as a retirement resort. Kelly planned to travel to England with Louise. They'd spent a short beach holiday after the French Open together. But when they got to De Gaulle Airport, they found that Peter Kong had insisted on buying Louise and her coach a first-class ticket. Kelly didn't see Louise until they were both in Eastbourne.

"Kong was in First Class too. He told me that the winner of the French Open has to travel First Class," Louise told Kelly when they met at Devonshire Park, where the tournament was to be held.

"Has he ever … you know … tried it on?" Kelly asked.

Louise shook her head. "Not with me. There were rumours about him and Maria, but then... Tetsuo says that Kong is simply a tennis fan who thinks that the women's game is more interesting than the men's."

Kelly wasn't convinced.

"Do you have a hitting partner yet?" Louise asked her.

"No. Mary said she was sorting something out, but she hasn't arrived."

"Play with me for a while."

The two girls knocked up. Grass was Kelly's favourite surface. She'd learnt to play on grass in her home town. Louise was less used to it. They didn't have grass courts in China. The two girls messed about on court. Kelly was having fun. Mary said that Eastbourne was the most relaxing part of the whole tour. Press pressure was off. The media were too busy thinking about Wimbledon to be any bother. There was a camaraderie between the players which wasn't possible at the big tournaments. *Maybe it's true*, thought Kelly. Then Louise's coach arrived.

"That's enough, ladies."

They stopped playing mid-point.

"You two are in the same half of the draw," Tetsuo pointed out. "You're rivals, until one of you gets knocked out. You shouldn't practise together."

So much for camaraderie. That was the trouble

with friendships on the tour, Kelly thought. Sooner or later, a game got in the way. The girls parted with a friendly smile and Kelly went to check the draw. She was in the same half as Louise and Lacy, but not Jessie-Ray. They couldn't meet before the final. Louise was seeded second, ahead of Jessie-Ray, who was fifth. Kelly was surprised to see that Elaine Murdoch was also seeded, at number ten. When she turned around, the South African player was standing next to her.

"Aren't you going to say congratulations?" Elaine asked.

"For what?"

"Haven't you been following the news since the French Open?"

"Not really," Kelly said. "I spent a few days on the beach with Louise."

Elaine smiled proudly.

"I won the DFS Classic at Edgbaston. What do you think?"

"That's brilliant. Congratulations. Who did you beat?"

"Almodovar."

The Spanish player was ranked just outside the top ten.

"Excellent."

"I beat Lacy Cannon in the semis, too – got my revenge on her. Watch out, Wimbledon. Here I come!"

Elaine walked off, pleased as punch. It was funny, Kelly thought, the way things turned around. She had written Elaine off recently, yet here she was, winning a tournament for the first time in over a year. Kelly guessed Eastbourne was going to be tough. She wanted another bite at Jessie-Ray, but her chances of getting that far were slim. She'd have to play as well as she had in the second set in Paris. Was that set a fluke, or could she really be that good, all the time?

"Surprise!"

Kelly turned round to see a tall, brown-haired Scot.

"Andrew! What are you doing here?"

"Mary hired me. You're my boss."

"Great!"

Andrew was the player who Kelly had played mixed doubles with in last year's Juniors at Wimbledon. He was also the nearest she'd come to a romance on the tour, until François.

"What are you doing now?" she asked him.

"I'm doing what we call A-levels – the things you need to get into university. I've got one exam left, but Mary persuaded me to work with you this week and at Wimbledon. She said it would be a surprise. Is it all right with you?"

"Of course it is!"

He was even better looking than she remembered. Kelly flashed him a big smile.

"Give me five minutes to get changed," he said. "I'll meet you on court."

Andrew worked Kelly hard. She needed practice. After Paris, she felt like the sparkle had gone out of her play. But it was odd seeing Andrew again. He'd grown and his face was now more like that of a man than that of a boy. Kelly could sense a restraint between them, not like the easy intimacy which she had established with François. She decided to avoid romance and concentrate on tennis. Andrew had his chance last year. Whether he was interested or not, Kelly didn't want to begin a relationship on the rebound.

After practice, Andrew had to go and revise. Kelly took a shower and decided to go for a walk. In Devonshire Park they were erecting the players' tent. As she watched this, Kelly bumped into Lacy Cannon.

"Hi!" Lacy beamed. "How are you?"

"Fine," Kelly assured her. "How about you? I heard you made it to the semis at Edgbaston."

Lacy nodded. "Just lucky."

Kelly did a double take. It wasn't like Lacy to admit that any success on her part was down to luck.

"I was even more surprised that Elaine won," Kelly added cautiously.

"Didn't you hear what happened?" Lacy asked.

"What do you mean?"

"There was a massive outbreak of food poisoning on the second day. Half the games were byes. I was OK until I got through the quarter-final, but it suddenly hit me the day before the semi. I should have dropped out, but I didn't want to give Elaine a free ride to the final, not after the way she treated me in Paris. I had to leave the court twice during the game to throw up."

"I'm sorry," Kelly said.

"Almodovar was still recovering when she lost to Elaine in the final," Lacy went on. "But you know what? Elaine claimed to have had a funny tummy herself, but she didn't play like she was in trouble once. Odd, huh?"

"Are you suggesting…?"

Lacy shrugged, but her expression was malicious.

"Some people are lucky. Some people have to make their own luck."

"What caused the food poisoning?" Kelly asked.

"Something in the buffet for the players on the night before the first round, probably. Elaine was there early." Lacy paused. "Anyway, I'm fine now. And we're both in the same half as Elaine. I hope one of us slaughters her, cuts her down to size."

"I guess," Kelly said. "Have you seen Louise? I was meant to be meeting her after practice."

Lacy paused.

"Last time I saw her, she wanted to get away from it all."

"Why?" Kelly asked.

Lacy looked uncomfortable.

"I'm not sure if I should say – she was getting some hassle."

"From Peter Kong?" Kelly guessed.

Lacy nodded.

"I guess she told you about him, huh? Kong wanted to take her to a car showroom, buy her a Mercedes as a reward for winning the French. Louise didn't want it. Said she didn't drive. If you ask me, she's crazy. Kong would have shipped it to Hong Kong. Louise could have sold it, or given it to her parents."

"Where did she go?"

"She said she was going to take a walk over on the cliffs by the beach."

As Kelly walked through the sleepy seaside town, she spotted Peter Kong. The millionaire, in his trademark linen jacket and an ugly pair of sunglasses, was walking straight towards her. Kelly ducked into a shop doorway, hoping that he wouldn't accost her. But Kong seemed preoccupied and walked straight by, without glancing to either side of him.

Kelly walked on. Maybe, she thought, Louise wants to be alone. Maybe I should steer clear of her for a while, as Tetsuo suggested, until one of us gets knocked out. But this wasn't a big tournament, like Wimbledon. It was a warm-up. Little depended on the result. Yet even less depended on the DFS tournament, the previous week, and Lacy had accused Elaine Murdoch of poisoning half the players. After Maria's death and Sue's accident, everybody was a little jumpy.

There was a stiff breeze coming in off the sea. Kelly got to the end of the promenade and the path stopped. There was a wooden barrier, followed by cliffs. Kelly was about to turn back when she saw Louise. Her friend was climbing up the tree-lined side of the cliff. That was Louise. In public, Kelly's friend was poised and polite. In private, she was impetuous and nosy. She liked to go places where you weren't supposed to go. Kelly decided to follow Louise and surprise her.

Seagulls squawked overhead. The climb was steeper than Kelly expected and she thought of turning back. After her training session this afternoon, she ought to be resting, not taking more exercise. But then she got to the top. It was windy but peaceful, and there was a good view out to sea and back at Eastbourne. Louise, however, was out of sight. Kelly walked. On the beach, several metres below, a middle-aged man in a tracksuit was whistling for his dog, who was on the rocks beneath the cliffs. When the whistling didn't work, he began shouting.

"Tricksy! Come on. Get out of there."

The dog barked, but didn't return. The man called again, in a more aggressive tone.

"Tricksy!"

How could you call a dog by such a silly name? Kelly wanted to know. She heard Tricksy make a whimpering noise. The dog's owner was losing his temper.

"Tricksy! Now!"

As she turned, Kelly glanced down to see if the animal was being obedient, hoping that it wasn't. It took her a moment to make out the dog, a golden retriever, which was near the base of the cliff. Its owner was stumbling his way across rocks to get to it. Kelly almost laughed. Then she saw why the dog was refusing to return. It had found something.

"Tricksy!"

Kelly went to the edge of the cliff. It was quite steep. She was close enough now to see what the dog had found, if the animal would just move away. The man in the tracksuit was panting. So was his dog. He had nearly reached the pet now, and his face was red with anger.

"Tri—" The man stopped, and froze to the spot. The dog backed away, still whimpering. Kelly's worst suspicions were confirmed. What the dog had found was a body: a dark-haired, badly-crumpled body wearing a blue blouse and a grey skirt.

And it looked an awful lot like Louise.

9

The beach was nearly empty. There was no way for Kelly to get down to Louise.

"Is she alive?" Kelly yelled to the man below. He didn't hear.

"Hey! You!"

The dog barked and the man looked up.

"Is she alive?" Kelly yelled again.

"Just about."

The wind barely carried the words back.

"I'm going for help. Stay with her," she shouted.

The words which came back sounded like "all right". Kelly ran as fast as she could, back towards the town. There were no houses nearby, certainly none of those British phone boxes like you used to see in old films. Kelly scrambled down where she had climbed up before, nearly falling several times. She must…

"Whooaa."

A man stepped out of the bushes, blocking her way. It was Peter Kong.

"What's wrong, Kelly?"

"I can't stop!" Kelly snapped at him, trying to push her way free, but Kong grabbed her arm.

"Hold it a second. You look like you've seen a ghost. Maybe I can help."

"I doubt it," Kelly snapped at him. "Someone's had an accident. I think it's Louise. She's fallen off the cliff."

"No!" Kong's face fell.

"I'm going for an ambulance."

"Wait." Kong reached into his pocket. The millionaire's concern seemed genuine, but Kelly remembered that it was a row with him which had driven Louise out here. "I've got a mobile phone," Kong said. "We can call one from here. Where did you say she was?"

Kelly told him. She listened as Kong described the location over the phone. He seemed to know the area awfully well, but then he had probably been to many previous tournaments here.

"Let's go down there."

They made their way along the stony beach. Kelly had to hold on to Kong's arm in a couple of places in order to keep her balance. They began running along the sand towards the accident. The nearer they got, the less doubt there was in Kelly's mind. It *was* Louise. When they got there her friend was still unconscious.

"Is she alive?"

The man in the tracksuit seemed uncertain. Kong fussed over Louise. Kelly pushed past the millionaire and checked Louise's pulse. It was there. Louise was breathing, but shallowly. Kong began to interrogate the man who'd found her. Kelly already knew that he'd seen nothing. She sat by her friend and held her hand. There was still a cool breeze, so she took off her cotton jumper and wrapped it around Louise's shoulders.

"It'll be all right," she repeated again and again. "Help's on the way. It'll be all right."

Yet, looking at her friend, and the awkward, unnatural way that her legs were splayed across the rocks, Kelly knew that – even if she lived – it would be a long, long time before everything was all right for Louise again.

After a while the helicopter came, landing as near to the rocks as it could. Louise was put on to a stretcher and carried carefully aboard. Kelly held Louise's hand while she was examined.

"How bad is it?" she asked the medic.

"Looks like the right leg's broken in several places. Not sure about the left. There are no obvious head injuries, but with a fall from that height, brain damage is a strong possibility."

"If there's anything ... anything at all that can be done for her," Kong interjected in a passionate voice, "I'll pay for it. Specialists ... I can fly them in from anywhere in the world. I can—"

"We have some very good doctors at the hospital," the pilot said sternly. "In this country, money's got nothing to do with the quality of care you receive after an accident. Now, let's get her there."

Kong was wise enough not to object.

The journey to the hospital seemed painfully slow. Louise didn't stir.

"How could it happen?" Kong kept asking. "She had the whole world at her feet. How could she let something crazy like this happen to her?"

The same thing was on Kelly's mind.

"What do you think?" Kong asked Kelly. "Suppose it wasn't an accident?"

Kelly looked him straight in the eye.

"We'll know when she recovers consciousness, won't we?" she said.

"What about Maria?" Kong asked. "Do you think that she killed herself?"

Kelly shrugged. She really didn't want to have this conversation now, here.

"You knew Maria. I didn't. What do you think?"

"I'll tell you," Kong said. "I'm sure she didn't. In fact…"

The noise increased as they landed at the hospital and the conversation ended. Louise was rushed to surgery.

"There's no point in either of you staying," one of the doctors said. "She'll be in there for hours."

"What are her chances?" Kelly asked.

"She'll live."

"But the tennis," Kong pleaded. "Will she—"

"Play again?" The doctor finished his sentence for him. "I've no idea. At the moment, I'm more concerned about whether she'll walk again. Are you family?" Kong shook his head.

"Then I've said too much already. Excuse me."

"Let's go," Kong told Kelly. "I hate hospitals."

"You go," Kelly said. "I'll wait."

"You can't. You have a match tomorrow," Kong lectured her.

"You don't think that I can play tennis after something like this has happened?" Kelly said bitterly.

"If you're a professional, you can. I saw you nearly beat Jessie-Ray in Paris. You looked like a professional to me."

Outside the hospital, the press were starting to arrive. A TV reporter recognized Kelly.

"Miss Christian, can you tell us what happened?"

"Eh…"

"No comment," Peter Kong said, waving the camera away. "Kelly's in shock after this terrible tragedy."

He pushed Kelly into the taxi and told it to wait.

"How about you, sir? Do you know what happened?"

Kelly couldn't hear properly, but it sounded to her like Kong was taking the credit for Louise's rescue. That was stupid. If anybody had found Louise, it was the golden retriever. But when Kong got into the taxi, she kept quiet. The millionaire asked her what hotel she was in. Kelly told him.

"We can't have you there. The media will be on to you constantly now. You need somewhere with better security. I'll sort something out."

"No," said Kelly, "Really. I'm all right."

As they drew up to the hotel entrance, Kong leant closer towards her, his arm brushing her bare, shivering leg.

"Let me help you," he said. "You could be a great player, Kelly. And I can be a very good friend."

"No," said Kelly. "Thank you, but no thanks."

And with that she hurried out of the car and into the hotel.

"Where have you been?" Mary snapped as Kelly walked into the room. "We were meant to be going over tactics as soon as I got here."

"Haven't you seen the news?"

"What news?" Mary remained impatient. "I've been briefing Andrew."

Kelly told her. Mary had to sit down.

"I don't believe it," she said. "First Sue. Then Maria. Now Louise. But surely it was an accident?"

"I don't know," Kelly said. "We won't know until she wakes up. Maybe not even then."

"Why not?"

"She might have brain damage. And she might not be able to walk."

Mary frowned.

"Has anyone contacted Louise's parents yet?"

"I guess Tetsuo will…"

"It'd be better coming from you," Mary said. "You've seen her. But don't mention brain damage, or anything about her not walking." Kelly was uncomfortable.

"Do I have to?" she asked Mary.

"You're her best friend. You've stayed with them. Her parents know you better than they know Tetsuo. They think of you as family, don't they?"

Kelly knew that her coach was right. She looked up the number in her diary, then picked up the phone to make the most difficult call of her life.

10

Kelly's mind was on other things when she played her first round match in the Volkswagen Cup. Louise still hadn't recovered consciousness. The doctors said she had severe concussion. They couldn't rule out brain damage. Kelly's opponent was Alice Ferrara who, like her, had just graduated from the Juniors. Kelly didn't tank, but she didn't try too hard either. She wanted to be with Louise, in hospital, not on court. She kept her concentration, though, and made few mistakes, winning 6-2, 6-2.

"It goes to show," Mary said afterwards. "Your game's coming together now. Even on an off-day you're very hard to beat."

*　　*　　*

After the game, Kelly went to visit Louise in hospital, as she'd planned. But she didn't stay long because Louise's parents had arrived. When Kelly got back to the hotel it was early evening. The police were there to interview her for a second time.

"You're sure you saw no one else during your walk?" Inspector Goad asked.

"Positive. Why? Do you think that she might have been pushed?"

The detective inspector shook her head.

"We doubt anyone would do such a thing in so public a place, but it's not a cliff which one can easily slip off. The drop's not big enough to attract potential suicides. They go further along, to Beachy Head."

"Why would Louise kill herself?" Kelly protested. "She had everything to live for!"

"True," the inspector said. "But why else would she climb on to that cliff? Out of curiosity, you say, or to get away from someone. Yet, if she didn't jump and she wasn't pushed, there has to be another reason for what happened." The inspector paused, then added, "You're certain that Mr Kong was behind you all the time?"

"Yes. I saw him in town before I set off on my walk."

Though, Kelly supposed, *he might have been able to get ahead of me*. Kong had been here before. He would know the short cuts. But Kelly didn't say this aloud.

"And..." the inspector said hesitantly, "you'll excuse me asking ... the two of you hadn't argued earlier, when her coach asked you to stop playing together?"

"No. Of course not. What was there to argue about?"

"Nothing, I'm sure. Thanks for your time, Miss Christian. Good luck tomorrow."

Kelly could hardly think about her second round match. She didn't even know who she was playing. Back in her room, rather than discuss tactics with Mary, she hung a "Do not Disturb" sign on her door and went to bed early, without eating.

It didn't work, though. She found it hard to sleep, and when she did drift off, her mind slipped immediately into nightmare. She was with Louise on the cliff and someone was trying to push her friend off.

"Not you," Louise was saying. "Why? Why?"

Then her friend fell, while Kelly watched, unable to interfere. The fall seemed to last for ever. Kelly was sure that any moment she too would meet the same fate. But, in the distance, an alarm was ringing. Someone was calling for help. Someone...

Kelly woke up and realized that it wasn't the alarm. It was her phone. She switched on the light and answered it. She heard Andrew's soft voice, with its distinctive accent. She called it Scottish, but he insisted it was "Scots".

"Kelly, I was about to hang up. Are you all right?"

"Yes. I was asleep."

"I'm sorry. I thought…"

"It's OK. I was having a bad dream. I'm glad you rang. What is it?"

"I was worried about you," Andrew said. "I haven't seen you since your match. I thought we were going to practise this evening."

"I know," Kelly said. "I just didn't feel up to it. The police were here and…"

Her voice trailed off.

"Have you eaten at least?" Andrew asked her.

"No." Kelly realized that she was ravenous.

"Have you?" she asked him.

"No. I was hoping that we could…"

"Is the hotel restaurant still open?"

"It closed at nine. I'll tell you what. Why don't I go out and get us a takeaway? I could give you time to get decent then bring it up to your room."

"That'd be great."

"What would you like?"

"You choose."

Kelly dressed quickly, dabbing perfume on her neck and arms. She liked Andrew. Without actually discussing it, he was sensitive to her situation. She didn't want to be seen in public any more than she could help at the moment – the press were bound to be prying into what had happened to Louise. Thinking of Louise, she rang the hospital – no change. Then she switched on the BBC news, which was nearly over. Louise's situation got thirty seconds.

"The French Open champion, Louise Chung, is still in a serious but stable condition after her fall from cliffs near Eastbourne yesterday. Detective Inspector Philippa Goad, who is heading the inquiry, has made an appeal for witnesses to the accident, which the police are currently at a loss to explain. At the Volkswagen Cup today, Miss Chung's opponent, Elaine Murdoch, was given a bye, while the woman she beat in the Paris final, Jessie-Ray Connor, continued her comeback with a swingeing 6-1, 6-0 defeat of the British player, Marie Dennis. Cricket, and in the Second Test…"

There was a knock at her door and Kelly turned the TV off. She could smell the meal before she let Andrew in: fish and chips. He had introduced her to this British delicacy last year. British chips were bigger than American fries and the cod in batter was heavenly.

"You read my mind," she said.

"The porter downstairs gave me a dirty look," Andrew laughed.

They ate the meal from its wrapping paper. Kelly explained to Andrew how she'd been interviewed by the police.

"Do you really think that something suspicious is going on?" Andrew asked.

"I guess we'll know when Louise wakes up," Kelly told him.

She didn't want to say *if*. Andrew looked thoughtful.

"Who do you suspect?" he asked.

"Suspect of *what*?"

"The way you're talking, it sounds like somebody's going round trying to bump off all of the top women tennis players."

"I never said that."

"You didn't have to. So, come on – who do you suspect?"

Kelly thought.

"It's silly, but … there's only one person who's profited from each of the accidents so far. She was in the same hotel as Maria, and she was supposed to play Louise today, and she was almost the only person not to get food poisoning in Edgbaston…"

Andrew nodded.

"I read about that. You're talking about the South African girl, Elaine."

"Yes. Elaine Murdoch. But she's only sixteen years old. I can't really see her as a murderer. It's not as though she benefited from Maria's death…"

Then Kelly remembered that Elaine had qualified for Paris as a result of Maria's death. And the player who knocked her out had been Louise.

She told Andrew this.

"What do you think we should do?" she asked him when she'd finished.

"It's not our problem. It's for the police. If you've worked out that she's a prime suspect, the police must have too."

"Are you sure? We're talking about two different countries. Also, both of the attacks looked like accidents."

"At least you're not in the same half of the draw as Elaine," Andrew said. "You can't be at risk unless you both get to the final."

"The way I feel at the moment," Kelly said, "I haven't a chance of getting through the second round. I haven't even checked who my opponent is."

Andrew squeezed her hand.

"Of course you can win," he told her. "You're playing great at the moment, a hundred times better than you were last year. In fact, everything…"

Kelly tried to smile gracefully, but felt herself blushing. Andrew too was going red as he stammered out the rest of the sentence.

"I mean … everything about you seems to be coming into bloom."

"Thank you."

Kelly wasn't in the mood for flirting, but Andrew didn't get the chance to press his suit further, for there was a knock on the bedroom door. It was Mary.

"You should be in bed," Kelly's coach lectured, "not eating late meals. It'll play havoc with your preparation tomorrow."

"I'll be fine," Kelly assured her. "Anyway, I've already had some sleep."

"I'll let you off this time," Mary said. "I've got good news – ICC Computers want you to sign an endorsement contract in time for Wimbledon."

"Computers – why would a computer company want to sponsor a tennis player?" Kelly asked.

"They'll give you a free computer – a portable PC for you to use on the road – a modem too. I expect they'll want to use it in their ads: 'I keep in touch with my courses wherever I am, thanks to ICC Computers.'"

"But I dropped out of school!"

"You intend to graduate high school some time, don't you? Do you want to know how much money we're talking?"

"Please."

Mary told her the sum. It was mind-bogglingly big.

"Don't let it go to your head," Kelly's coach warned her. "There'll be plenty more bigger and better contracts to come if you keep playing the way you have been doing."

She turned to Andrew.

"Now, come on, young man. I told you when I gave you this job – no late-night visits to your boss's bedroom, remember?"

Andrew stood up sheepishly. Mary gave Kelly a playful wink.

"I have revision to do anyway," he said.

"How's Louise?" Mary asked when he'd gone.

Kelly told her.

"I know it's hard, but try to put her to the back of your mind until the next game's over."

When Mary left, Kelly went straight to bed, but she could never sleep just after eating, so she turned the TV on. There wasn't much choice: current affairs, cricket or American reruns. At one thirty, when *LA Law* had finished on Channel Four, she finally turned off the TV and the lights. She managed six hours of shallow sleep, then rang the hospital to ask after Louise. No change. There was nothing for Kelly to do but shower, get dressed and try to carry on.

11

"Who's that?" Kelly asked Lacy Cannon when they bumped into each other on the practice courts. "Your new hitting partner?"

The man she was pointing to wore a dark suit and looked like a body-builder.

"Hardly," Lacy said. "He's my bodyguard."

"Isn't that a bit paranoid?" Kelly asked.

"After what happened to Louise? You tell me."

She had a point, Kelly realized. But there was no way that she could afford a bodyguard. Rich, leading players had had them for years. But Lacy was only the same age as Kelly. They were ranked in the eighties. If Lacy felt at risk...

"Who're you playing?" Kelly asked.

"Some British girl who's number 298 or there-abouts."

"You ought to watch out. A lot of them are good on grass."

"Sure."

Lacy went off to join her hitting partner. Her dark-suited shadow followed close behind.

"Ready?"

It was a pleasure to see Andrew's warm, smiling face.

"Ready as I'll ever be."

"Sleep well?"

"Not bad, considering."

As they went out to play, Kelly passed Elaine Murdoch. The South African girl gave her a bright, cheery grin. Kelly smiled back, trying to cast from her mind the dark suspicions of the night before. This afternoon, she had to play Petra Gordon, the new number two seed.

"Remember," Mary told Kelly just before she went out to play, "on any given day, someone in the top hundred can beat someone in the top ten. Play the way you've been playing lately, and you've got a good chance."

"I'll do my best," Kelly said.

On court, she followed her game plan. Gordon was a baseline player, so Kelly came into the net as much as she could. She got caught out a few times by well-timed lobs which she couldn't get back for, but her serve held up well and the top spin she kept putting on her returns clearly bothered Gordon. At 6-6, they went into a tie-break.

On another day, perhaps, Kelly would have choked. But, today, tennis seemed so insignificant, so silly a pastime when her friend was critically ill. Kelly couldn't become self-conscious. She concentrated on every shot and won 7-6. Gordon won the second set, 6-4, outplaying Kelly on the crucial points.

In the final set, Kelly competed for everything. She won her serve easily and had a break point against Gordon in the second game. In the fourth, she broke her, but Gordon immediately broke back. The next four games each went to deuce, but the result went with serve. After an hour and a half's play, it was 5-4 to Kelly, with Gordon serving.

Gordon's first serve was an ace. Kelly managed a good stop volley to even the score on the second point. Then Gordon got her out of position and took the lead again. Kelly evened the score with the best cross-court volley she could remember playing, which Gordon hammered into the net. This was the time when the number two seed needed an ace, but her serve was fractionally out. Kelly tried to focus. She had to exploit Gordon's weaker, second serve. But this serve wasn't weak: it tore to Kelly's left, testing her backhand.

"Out. Thirty-forty."

Gordon had double faulted. It was break point

and match point. The next serve was more tentative. Kelly hammered it to the far left of the court and hurried to the net. Gordon's return was reasonable, but Kelly was in the perfect position. She smashed the ball and the audience began to roar.

"You played superbly," Petra said, holding out her hand. "Never let up."

"Thanks."

As she shook the umpire's hand and walked off court, it slowly dawned on Kelly: she had beaten the number two seed. She was in with a chance.

When Kelly visited the hospital she found that Louise had recovered consciousness briefly, but was now sleeping again.

"Did she say how it happened?" Kelly asked Mrs Chung.

"No," Louise's mother said. "I don't think she knows what's going on, which is probably for the best. The doctors want to operate again tomorrow. Only then will they know how full a recovery she can make."

As she was leaving the hospital, Kelly saw Peter Kong, bearing flowers. He congratulated her on her win.

"Listen," he said. "If you won't let me move you to a better hotel, at least let me hire a bodyguard for you."

"I don't need a bodyguard."

"I expect that's what Louise thought," Kong said quietly, before going inside to deliver his flowers.

Kelly was still thinking about Kong's offer as she got back to the hotel. The hotel was on a one-way street. The taxi dropped her at the end of it, on the other side from the hotel. Kelly paid, then the taxi drove off. She crossed the empty street.

"Look out!"

From out of nowhere, a motorbike screeched down the road in the wrong direction. It was heading straight at Kelly. She jumped out of the way, but was jostled as the hot, speeding weapon passed her. It shot down the road, round the corner and out of sight.

Kelly picked herself up off the floor before another vehicle could come along, or the bike return. She was shaken but, thankfully, uninjured. Then she looked around for the person who'd warned her. There was no one there.

"Did you see that?" she asked the receptionist in the hotel.

"What?"

"Never mind."

There was an electric kettle in her room. Kelly made herself a cup of hot, sweet tea. Then she put on the television. When the cricket finished, they showed highlights of that day's play at Eastbourne.

First came Jessie-Ray, easily defeating Karla Zbignew. Then they showed the final two games of Kelly's match.

"A very impressive performance," said the commentator. "We didn't get to talk to Kelly after the match, but we did speak to her coach, former champion Mary Porter, who won this event twice herself. Mary, a very plucky performance?"

"Yes, indeed. Especially since, as you know, Kelly is worried sick about her friend, Louise Chung, who she's visiting in hospital as we speak. I was delighted with Kelly's play today. She's developing so quickly. I really do think that she's got the potential to be a world beater."

"And her opponent in the next round is Elaine Murdoch, who won at Edgbaston on Sunday. A tough draw?"

Elaine. Kelly felt her heart sink. But Mary spoke cheerfully.

"Kelly and Elaine are friends. I expect it'll be a close match. But if Kelly plays like she played today, she can win it."

There was a familiar knock on Kelly's door: Andrew. She let him in.

"So you've heard?" he said, pointing at the screen. Kelly nodded.

"And Elaine's heard, too," she said, pointing at the scuff marks on her jeans.

"How do you mean?"

Kelly told him. As she did, Andrew became angry. She felt uneasy when he got this way, even though he was on her side.

"I guess I'd better go to the police," she said.

"And tell them what? You have no evidence against Elaine. If she arranged the attack, she'll have a good alibi for what happened today, and for what happened to Louise on Sunday."

"Maybe you're right," Kelly said. "But I think we should check."

"Sure," Andrew told her. "And, from now on, I'm not letting you out of my sight. You need a bodyguard."

"Yes," said Kelly bashfully. "I guess I do."

Their eyes met. His head inclined towards hers. Before Kelly had decided whether to let him kiss her, there was a knock on the door.

"You two ready to eat dinner?" Mary asked from the corridor. "We have a game plan to discuss."

Andrew's lips brushed Kelly's, but the kiss didn't happen. It lingered in the air like a promise for the future.

12

"What's with the attitude?" Elaine asked Kelly, as they walked out on to court. "You haven't said two words to me. Are you trying to psych me out or something?"

Kelly mumbled an inaudible reply. She had no real evidence against Elaine, but found it hard to be civil to someone she suspected of such violent acts.

"If you're going to be like that…" Elaine muttered.

Then they both smiled at each other because the cameras were on them. They began to knock up. Watching Elaine, with her curly, carefully-coiffured hair, Kelly reminded herself that she meant to smarten up her image before Wimbledon. She won the toss, and elected to serve.

Elaine played her normal game. Whatever she had that enabled her to win in Edgbaston, she didn't have this afternoon. Today, Kelly had the killer instinct. She won the first game to love and only allowed Elaine one point on her own serve. She annihilated the South African girl 6-0, 6-1; Elaine took the penultimate game, saving herself the humiliation of a double bagel. When the two girls shook hands at the end of the match, Elaine avoided Kelly's eyes. *That'll teach you,* Kelly thought. But, as they entered the locker-room, she saw that her opponent was in tears. Could this vulnerable-looking sixteen-year-old really have been behind the things which had been happening off court?

"You were superb," Andrew told her in the players' tent. "Every shot you went for seemed to work."

"I was focused," Kelly said. "I was angry."

"Whatever," Mary told her. "You're in the quarter finals."

Lacy, too, had made it to the quarter-finals.

"How's Louise?" she asked.

"I don't know. I'm on my way to see her."

"Give her my best, if she's awake."

"Sure."

Louise wasn't awake when Kelly arrived. She was recovering from her operation.

"The surgeon thinks it was a success," Mr Chung

told Kelly. "She says that there's a good chance – with the right training and physiotherapy – that Louise will be able to play tennis again next year."

"That's wonderful," Kelly said.

Mrs Chung asked Kelly about her match and congratulated her on her win. This embarrassed Kelly. It ought to have been Louise out there on the courts, enjoying her first flush of real success. As it turned out, she was lucky to be alive.

The next day, Lacy played first. She had two set points against the number five seed, Kieslowski, but lost on the tie-break, eventually going out in straight sets. Kelly's opponent was Helena Bogdanovitz, from the Czech Republic, who was seeded seventh. After beating Petra Gordon, Kelly felt that she could beat anyone. She took the first set easily. Bogdanovitz managed to hold on to the second, winning 6–4. But in the final set, Kelly was all over her, and won 6–1.

The semi-final, the following day, was an anti-climax. Krystal Kieslowski was carrying an injury, and Kelly won easily, 6–3, 6–1. She was through to the final – her first ever final. She hoped Louise would be conscious so that she could tell her about it in the hospital tonight. But, first, she decided to stay and watch her two potential opponents.

Jessie-Ray Connor was playing the Japanese number four seed, Myu Hitaki. The young Japanese woman tried hard, but was quickly overwhelmed. Jessie-Ray was playing with the sort of form she had shown as a sixteen-year-old, running her opponent ragged. Her victory was even more convincing than Kelly's had been. It was all over in fifty minutes. On the way off the court, Jessie-Ray spotted Kelly in the audience. She smiled in a friendly way, then made a little gesture with two of her fingers: that of a handgun, blowing somebody away. Kelly half grinned as though she appreciated the joke. Inside herself, however, she didn't think that it was very funny.

Louise smiled when Kelly walked into her private room. They hugged.

"Mum says you've been to see me every day."

Kelly nodded.

"I've been so worried about you."

"They say I'll be able to play again," Louise said. "Next year, probably."

"That's great."

Louise shrugged.

"Well, we'll see."

Kelly's friend was always more fatalistic than she was. Her attitude was always "if it happens, it happens", whereas Kelly wanted everything, now. She wondered how she'd cope if she was in Louise's position.

"Tell me about your games," Louise said.

"Not until you tell me how you fell off that cliff."

The smile left Louise's face.

"I've spent the last hour going over it with the police," she said. "I don't remember. The last thing I remember is walking near the cliffs."

"You don't remember going over the barrier, climbing up through the trees?"

"Not really. You know, I have this vague sense that I was trying to get away from someone or something but…"

"You don't remember falling?"

"No. The doctors say I could have had an epileptic fit. I've never had one before but sometimes they don't hit people until their teens. They're doing tests. The more likely explanation is that the trauma was so great I've blocked it out of my memory. The police want me to undergo hypnosis to see if I remember anything else, but I'm not sure."

"But if someone tried to kill you…"

Louise shook her head.

"Probably it was an accident. Why look for the most sinister explanation for things that happen?"

She paused, then added, "Though there is one strange thing which keeps going through my mind."

"What?"

"The last thing I remember, before coming round in hospital … I was walking along the cliff top and I smelt something, a perfume, close to me – it smelt

expensive, unusual … maybe I turned round…"
Her words faltered, as Kelly's mind raced. "That's all."

"Would you recognize the perfume again?" Kelly asked.

"I doubt it. Though Inspector Goad said that our memory of smell is one of the strongest we have. But … who knows. Tell me about your tournament so far."

Reluctantly, Kelly told Louise the story, but her mind was elsewhere. Soon a doctor came and warned Louise about overtiring herself. Kelly used this as her excuse for leaving.

"I'll come and see you tomorrow," she said.

"I'll tell you how to beat Jessie-Ray," Louise promised.

It was weird. Kelly was in her first final, yet she'd hardly thought about it. Right now, she was more concerned about the perfume which Louise smelt before falling (or being pushed) off the cliff. When she got in the taxi, instead of asking for her own hotel, she asked to be taken to the Grand, the five-star hotel where the most successful players stayed.

Once she got inside the foyer, Kelly had no idea what she was going to do. She wanted to know what kind of perfume Elaine Murdoch had in her room. If memory served her right, Elaine should be playing doubles at the moment. She was in the quarter-finals. If Kelly knew what room Elaine was staying in, maybe she could get the key. But, even then, whoever was on reception might recognize Kelly, and realize that she wasn't staying in the hotel. It wasn't worth the risk.

Kelly saw someone she knew entering the hotel. It was Lacy. She was wearing a cotton polka dot summer dress which looked brand new and, judging from the bags she was carrying, she had spent the afternoon shopping. There was no time for Kelly to get out of the way, so she beamed a big smile at her fellow American.

"Kelly!" Lacy said. "Great win today! I'm so proud of you. What are you doing here? Decided to move up in the world?"

Kelly shook her head.

"I came to see you."

They were interrupted when a boy came in from the street and asked both girls for their autographs. It was only as they were signing that Kelly noticed Lacy's bodyguard, waiting a few yards away, ready to pounce if there was any trouble. Should she take up Peter Kong's offer and let him provide her with a bodyguard?

"Shall we go for a drink in the bar?" Lacy suggested when the autograph-seeker had gone.

"Why don't we go up to your room?" Kelly said. "We won't be pestered there."

"Good idea. Then I can dump my shopping," Lacy said. "These are all presents. My parents are coming over to watch Wimbledon. Actually, you're lucky to find me. I was due to check out this morning, but decided to stay on an extra day."

"I'm glad you did," Kelly said.

Lacy's bodyguard saw them up to the room, then waited outside.

"Is he in the room next door?" Kelly asked, wondering if she could get to the subject of which players were staying in which rooms.

"No," Lacy said. "The rooms on this side of the hall are far too expensive. He's across the hall. Jessie-Ray's in the room next door."

"Is Elaine staying on this floor too?" Kelly asked, hoping that the question didn't sound too incongruous. Tennis players weren't usually interested in each other's hotel rooms.

"Yeah, she's another two doors down from Jessie-Ray."

Kelly calculated. This was the second room on the corridor, so the rooms which Lacy was referring to must be to the right. Now Kelly knew Elaine's room number. All she had to do was find a way to get in there.

"Why were you coming to see me?" Lacy asked. "A social visit? How's Louise?"

Kelly told Lacy about Louise, all the time trying to figure out a reason why she might have come to see Lacy. Luckily, Lacy provided it for her.

"I guess Louise's accident made you consider what I was saying about us playing doubles together, huh?"

Kelly smiled with relief.

"Yes. That's right."

"You two had your names down for Wimbledon, didn't you?"

"Yes, but I guess they'll have scrubbed us by now. Who were you supposed to be playing with?"

"I'm afraid," Lacy said, "that I agreed last weekend to play with Jessie-Ray. Sorry."

"Oh, it's all right," Kelly said. "It was just a thought, really. Maybe some other time."

"Sure," Lacy said. "And I'm glad you asked me. You know, I wish we knew each other better. It's nice having people you can gossip with on the tour. I got on with Elaine OK for a while, but then we had that stupid row. You and Louise always seem a bit aloof."

"We don't mean to be," Kelly assured her.

"I like the look of your new hitting partner. What's his name?"

"Andrew."

"He's neat. Are you sleeping with him?"

"No!"

Kelly was shocked by the frankness of the question.

"I'll bet it won't be long," Lacy said. "I wish I

had a hitting partner his age. You know, Chuck is nearly forty."

Chuck was Lacy's coach and hitting partner.

"Pity Andrew isn't a pro," Lacy went on. "You could play mixed doubles together at Wimbledon."

"Pity," Kelly agreed.

They talked a while longer then Kelly remembered that she had to go. She knocked on Elaine's door as she was leaving. No answer. Then she tried the handle. It was locked, of course. She would have to think of a way to get in there tomorrow.

13

Kelly spent the evening practising her serve and doing exercises. She was playing better than ever before, but against Connor, physical strength would be important, too. Kelly worked out a lot. The muscles in her arms were constantly growing. It was a tension for women players. Kelly didn't want to look like a body-builder, or a bull. Yet the stronger she was, the better she played.

"Your serve's much bigger," Andrew said, coming up to the net when she'd aced him for the first time. "Who've you been working on it with?"

"Oh, you know, Mary … and there was this guy in France, a junior."

"Like me, huh? I guess you get through a lot of young guys."

There was a flirtatious smile on his face as he said this.

"Less than you'd think," Kelly replied.

"What're you doing later on?" he asked.

After the day she'd had, Kelly was considering an early night, but tomorrow was a rest day before the final. She could stay up late if she wanted.

"I don't have any plans," she told Andrew. "How about you?"

"Me neither. I'm meant to be revising for my final Chemistry exam next Friday. I was kind of expecting to be home by now."

"I'm sorry my success has got in the way of your exam schedule," Kelly said, half-jokingly. "Would you like me to help you revise, ask you practice questions or something?"

"I think you'd be more of a distraction," Andrew said with a sheepish grin.

"Oh," said Kelly. "Why's that?"

They were standing very close to each other, with only the net between them. It was a hot afternoon, but Kelly could still feel the warmth of Andrew's breath as he struggled for a reply.

"You know," he said.

Then, before she could stop him, Andrew leant forward and kissed her lightly on the lips.

"There's something for you to think about," he said.

* * *

"Was that a kiss I observed on the court earlier?" Mary asked when Kelly was alone with her. Mary didn't miss much.

"Just a friendly peck," Kelly replied, embarrassed.

"Remember," Mary said, "Andrew's your employee. And he's temporary. If you continue doing well, we'll hire you a longer-term hitting partner."

"And suppose I want Andrew?"

Mary's voice became more maternal.

"I doubt that he'd be available, Kelly. He's only eighteen. He wouldn't want to play second fiddle to a girl even younger than he is. It would only lead to resentment. I've seen it happen before."

"What are you trying to say?" Kelly asked, not hiding the irritation in her voice.

"Don't get emotionally involved," Mary replied. "There's a time for boys, and it isn't just before the first final of your professional career."

"You didn't object to my getting involved with François."

"François was a friendship you made. You weren't paying him. Are you going out with Andrew tonight?"

"He's revising for his exam on Friday."

"Ah, yes. And if he passes he goes to university."

"I guess."

Andrew could have a normal life, Kelly realized. He could find himself a normal girl who didn't spend three-quarters of the year travelling around the world, staying in hotel rooms. Until recently she'd been struggling to make ends meet. But if she could play consistently, big money beckoned. Get into the top twenty, and she could make millions. It would make a huge difference to her family. She could repay the sacrifices they'd made to put her on the tour. All right, maybe it would be hard for her to have a normal relationship. She would have to wait until her thirties, or until injury ended her career, before she had children of her own. But the prizes were high.

Then Kelly thought about Mary. Her coach was sitting opposite her, eating in silence. She was thirty-four now and had never married. Her child-bearing years were slipping away. Tennis was her life. Would Kelly end up like her, devoting the rest of her life to what was, when it came down to it, just another sport?

"Penny for them."

"I was thinking about Jessie-Ray," Kelly lied. "You used to know her. What's she really like?"

"We were never that close," Mary said. "I'm so much older than her. She was just a kid – ambitious, obsessed with the game, pushed by her parents, the usual story. She'd do anything to win, and she had quite a temper when she was losing. But you've seen that on TV."

"Do you really think that I can be as good as her?" Kelly asked.

"I think that you can be better than she was, given time. Whereas she'll never be as good as she once was. She can't get back those five years."

"I think I'll have an early night," Kelly said later, leaving her dessert unfinished.

"Fine by me," Mary told her. "I'll see you in the morning."

Kelly only remembered as she left that she still hadn't told Mary about the motorbike attack. The incident was so similar to Sue Murray's accident. Would Mary advise her to tell the police? Kelly had no description of the motorcyclist. She hadn't seen the number-plate, only a grey blur. She would discuss it with Andrew later.

In her room, Kelly didn't undress. She made enough noise for Andrew, two doors down, to hear her. He didn't come. In a way she was relieved. She was tired and lonely and needed some attention. Yet Mary was right. A relationship with Andrew wouldn't be wise. She'd be better off talking to someone who really knew her. But what close friends did she really have? Louise was in hospital and François had dumped her. Kelly wanted to ring home, but it was mid-afternoon there. No one would be in. She lay down on the bed and cried herself to sleep.

The next thing she knew it was morning. She'd slept in her clothes. Kelly had a shower and was drying her hair when there was a knock on her door. She pulled her dressing-gown around her and let Andrew in.

"I came to see you last night," he said.

"I must have fallen asleep," Kelly admitted. "I'm sorry. I was exhausted. Have you had breakfast?"

He nodded.

"Mary had to see CBS about doing some commentary for them at Wimbledon. She told me what I should go over with you. We're to meet her for lunch."

"Fine. I'll grab a bowl of cereal downstairs. We can be at the courts in twenty minutes."

"OK."

He was meant to go now but seemed in no hurry to leave. Give him half an excuse to stay and anything might happen – if she wanted it to happen. But Kelly had a final to prepare for. And there was another, even more important task.

"There's something else I'd like you to help me with," she said. "Something private."

"Sounds intriguing."

"I'll tell you about it on the way over there."

Andrew left and Kelly changed straight into her practice gear. After bolting down breakfast, she rang to check on Louise, then went over to Devonshire Park. On the way, she told Andrew about the perfume and her plan to search Elaine's room. He listened carefully.

"What will you do if you get in there?" Andrew asked.

"I'll check the bathroom, see what perfume she wears and, if there's anything unusual, I'll take a dab of it to see if Louise recognizes the smell."

"Sounds a bit far-fetched to me," he complained.

"Got any better ideas?"

"Yes," Andrew said as he drove into the competitors' car-park. "Leave the investigation to the police and concentrate on your match tomorrow."

"Louise is my best friend," Kelly protested. "And the police are treating her fall like it was an accident."

"I'd say it was much more likely that it was an accident than that Elaine Murdoch caused it," Andrew said. "But I'll help you if you want. We have to be careful, though. When's Elaine playing today?"

"She's on first. Her doubles semi-final isn't due to start until two," Kelly said. "I reckon that the best time to get into her room would be when they're making up the beds. What we ought to do is wait until she shows up here to practise, then go straight over to the Grand."

"That sounds like a good plan to me," Andrew agreed.

But he still looked dubious.

They practised hard, taking frequent breaks to see if Elaine Murdoch had arrived to practise with her doubles partner. Just before eleven, she did, walking straight past Kelly and Andrew without a greeting. She hadn't forgiven Kelly the hammering she gave her in the quarter-finals.

"Come on," Kelly said when Elaine was out of sight. "Let's get over there."

Their plan depended on a maid showing up to clean Elaine's room and leaving the door open. Andrew would be look-out. Kelly's excuse for being there was that she thought she'd lost a brooch in Lacy's room the previous evening. If this ruse didn't work, they'd have to find a way of getting the key to Elaine's room.

They made it up to the third floor without being seen. Kelly was worried about bumping into Lacy, but a quick glance showed her door open and the room empty. She'd already checked out. Elaine's door, however, was closed and locked. The maid's trolley was at the other end of the corridor.

"Come on," said Andrew.

They went back down to the lobby again. It was twenty past eleven and they were meant to be meeting Mary for lunch at one. Suppose Elaine's room had already been cleaned? It was a chance they would have to take. Andrew and Kelly hid in a charity shop, where no one would expect to see a tennis star. Kelly flicked through dusty books and old LP records in their cardboard sleeves. Did people still have record players? She found a copy of a novel by Martina Navratilova, one of her biggest heroes. She was about to buy it when she realized that doing so would draw attention to herself, the last thing she wanted.

"Come on," said Andrew. "It's been fifteen minutes. Let's go back."

They took the lift up to Elaine's floor. This time, Kelly saw with relief, the maid's trolley had moved further down the corridor. The door to Elaine's room, together with that of Jessie-Ray and the one in between, was open.

"Quick," she told her hitting partner. "Keep watch."

Andrew stood just to the side of the lift, where he could duck out of sight of the corridor. If someone came he was to shout "hurry up, or we'll be late" and Kelly would beat a hasty retreat from Elaine's room. She only needed to spend a few seconds in the en-suite bathroom, looking for perfume. It should be easy. But when she peeked into the room, the maid was there, making the bed. Kelly went back to Andrew.

"Come on," he said. "This is making me nervous. Let's get out of here."

"We have to be patient," she told him.

The lift went and came up again. Kelly prayed that it would not stop on this floor. How would she explain her presence if someone she knew got out? But she should be safe. Most of the players were on court. The lift went by. The maid came out of Elaine's room and went two doors down, into Jessie-Ray's. Kelly heard the sound of a vacuum cleaner being switched on.

"Go for it!" Andrew said.

Kelly hurried down the corridor into Elaine's room. There was no perfume in the bathroom, so she checked the room itself. There were three bottles beneath the mirror on the dresser: Chanel no.5, Coco and Dior. None of them was strong and each scent would be familiar to Louise. Kelly had drawn a blank. If Elaine had been the heavily-perfumed assailant, she must have got rid of the evidence.

Kelly left the room. The maid was vacuuming the neighbouring room now, but the door to Jessie-Ray's room was still open. More out of curiosity than suspicion, Kelly went in. The room was spartan: the only personal items on display were a leather-bound bible and a photograph of Jessie-Ray's son. Kelly checked the bathroom. There was some Oil of Ulay and two expensive bottles: an elegant, pyramid-shaped one of L'Eau D'Issy and a blue, round bottle of something called Baudelaire. Kelly took a dab of each with separate hand-kerchiefs which she put in plastic bags, one in each pocket. Then she turned to leave. The door slammed shut.

"What are *you* doing here?"

Kelly found herself facing Jessie-Ray Connor. The American star was glaring at her. Kelly was lost for words.

"I … um … thought I left my brooch in here when I used the bathroom last night."

"Last night? When were you in here last night?"

"Well … this is Lacy's room, isn't it?"

Jessie-Ray shook her head.

"This is my room. I don't like it when people invade my privacy. And I have more reason than most."

"I'm sorry. It looked empty to me. I knew Lacy checked out this morning and assumed it was hers."

Jessie-Ray still wasn't satisfied.

"What are you doing with that perfume bottle?"

"It's unusual," Kelly tried to lighten the tone of her voice, get friendly. "I was just taking a look. Where did you get it?"

"Paris. I've been using it for years. Now would you get out of here, *please*? I don't think it's appropriate for us to meet the day before the final, especially given all the peculiar things that have been going on."

She said the last few words with a sarcastic, suspicious tone.

"Sure," Kelly said, like she was talking to a teacher who had caught her cheating in a test. "Sorry to disturb you."

Kelly left quickly, deeply embarrassed. Jessie-

Ray was once one of her heroes, and now she had made herself look like a fool in front of her. Andrew was waiting by the lift. They got in.

"I couldn't make you hear me over the sound of the vacuum cleaner," he said. "Did you find anything?"

"Maybe. I won't know until I see Louise later."

Before that, Kelly had to practise. It was nearly six before she got to the hospital. Louise was feeling better, and full of advice about how to tackle Jessie-Ray.

"Try to keep changing your game. She's very intelligent. She looks for a pattern and tries to exploit it. Don't give her the chance. Be unpredictable. If you play well, you can beat her."

Kelly knew that this was good advice, but it wasn't easy to follow. Once you were on court, it was hard to take complete control of a game, no matter how brilliant your match plan was.

"Thanks," she told her friend. "Now there's something I want you to do. A kind of test."

Louise looked bemused.

"What?"

"Close your eyes and smell these."

Louise looked annoyed.

"I did all this for Inspector Goad yesterday. We got nowhere."

"Have another go, for me, please."

"If you insist."

Kelly took the first handkerchief, with the L'Eau D'Issy, from the air-tight bag which she'd sealed it into. Louise took one sniff.

"No."

Kelly waited a moment for the air to clear, then handed Louise the second handkerchief, the one impregnated with Baudelaire. Louise smelt it, then smelt again. She opened her eyes.

"That's it," she said. "That's the one the attacker was wearing. Where did you get it?"

Kelly told her.

14

"I have to go to the police," Kelly said.

Mary shook her head. She'd listened carefully to Kelly explaining her ideas about the attacks on tennis players, including the motorbike which nearly ran her over and the perfume in Jessie-Ray's room. But Mary wasn't impressed.

"Bring in the police the night before a final? Forget it. You may be right about Jessie-Ray pushing Louise off that cliff – all those drugs she took in her teens may have done something odd to her mind, I don't know – but there could be an innocent explanation too. Who knows what went on in Louise's mind after the accident? The simple truth is – she can't remember what happened that day. If you accuse Jessie-Ray tonight it will look like you're setting her up. Let Louise tell the police when she's ready. They'll get Jessie-Ray if she's guilty."

"I guess you're right," Kelly said. "But it makes me angry that someone could be so ruthless ... so evil ... so..."

"This is top level sport," Mary told her. "There are millions of dollars at stake. People do crack under the pressure. I don't want it happening to you. So let's forget this Nancy Drew stuff and work on your game."

"I'm going to beat her," Kelly asserted.

"I'm glad you're thinking positively," her coach said.

"No, I'm not thinking positively," Kelly insisted. "I'm thinking destructively. If it's the last thing I do, I'm going to beat Jessie-Ray tomorrow."

Mary stopped smiling. She could see how serious Kelly was, how much the attack on Louise had affected her.

"All right," she said. "Let's work out how you're going to do it."

Before she went to bed that night, Kelly spoke to her parents in Massachusetts.

"I'm really sorry we can't be there," her mother said. "We'll be thinking of you every minute. You ring us the moment you get off court – win or lose."

"I will."

Her father and brother came on. Both asked about Louise, but it was hard for them to be very sympathetic because they hardly knew her. Kelly didn't tell them her suspicions about Jessie-Ray's involvement in the "accidents". She didn't want to worry them unduly. When they had rung off, and she was alone in her room, Kelly felt emotional and very lonely.

She heard Mary's knock on the door.

"You should be in bed now," Mary said. "Big day tomorrow."

"I've only just finished talking to my folks. Don't worry, I'm going to bed."

"Sleep well."

Kelly was half-undressed when there was another knock on the door. She opened it a crack. Andrew stood there, his hair a little tousled, smiling awkwardly.

"I thought I heard you moving about," he said a little nervously. "I just wanted to say 'good night'."

Kelly opened the door a little wider. She wanted so much to be held tonight. She didn't want to be on her own, facing the fears which came when the lights went out. The look on his face told her how much he wanted to be invited inside. But something made her hold off. She leant forwards and kissed Andrew on the cheek.

"Thanks for helping today," she said softly. "G'night."

*   *   *

It was a brilliant British summer's afternoon. Hot, but not too hot. Seagulls flew overhead. They said that the grass at Eastbourne was better than the grass at Wimbledon. It was certainly better than the grass at home. When you got down on your knees to play a shot it was softer, more supple. This was a completely different game to clay or concrete, and Kelly was good at it.

"Two minutes, ladies."

In the locker-room, Kelly and Jessie-Ray had ignored each other. Now, as they knocked up, they had to make a pretence of being civil. Did Jessie-Ray know why Kelly had been in her room yesterday? Had the police already interviewed the other finalist about her whereabouts the afternoon that Louise fell from the cliff? Kelly didn't know.

"One minute."

Devonshire Park was overflowing. Mary said that there was more media interest than ever before. Jessie-Ray's return and Kelly's emergence as a highly-promising player were talked about in the papers. One said that there was "a new dawn for women's tennis", promising "the most exciting Wimbledon for years".

"Mrs Connor to serve."

The ball shot through the air and Kelly froze for a second. *She wasn't ready for this*. Her arm reached out, but the racket didn't connect.

"Fault."

Kelly breathed a sigh of relief. The second service was shorter and Kelly hit a cross-court volley which caught Jessie-Ray out of position, forcing her to hit the net.

"Love-fifteen."

Kelly only scored one more point in the game, but she made Jessie-Ray run a lot. Her opponent couldn't be as match fit as Kelly was, and Kelly wanted to use the advantage of her youth. She held her serve and the next four games followed the same pattern. The two players were getting the measure of each other. Kelly varied her shots, trying to remain unpredictable, at the same time trying to gauge where Jessie-Ray was weakest. But it was hard to concentrate. So much was at stake. The prize money was the least of it. Mary was fielding constant enquiries about endorsement deals. If Kelly won, the offers would pour in.

The seventh game of any set was always crucial, especially if the scores were tied. Break your opponent on this game and it was hard, psychologically, for them to come back. Lose, and you would soon be in the position of having to keep holding your serve to stay in the match.

As Jessie-Ray slammed her serve to Kelly's backhand, Kelly tried to lift her game a gear. She returned long, then came into the net with a stop volley which Jessie-Ray couldn't reach. On the next point, she lobbed her, taking a love-thirty lead. Jessie-Ray won the next two points with vicious serves, but then Kelly went ahead again, approaching the net and smashing Jessie-Ray's topspun return beyond her reach. Break Point.

Jessie-Ray served hard, yet Kelly got it back and came into the net once more. But she had done this once too often. Jessie-Ray lobbed her, forcing Kelly to run back. She got the ball back, but left her opponent with an easy smash.

"Deuce."

Kelly got an advantage on the next point, but Jessie-Ray held on to win the next three, and the game. Kelly couldn't believe it. She'd been so sure that she was going to win the game. Now she had to go straight on and win her own serve.

Jessie-Ray was pumped and ready, while Kelly's confidence was sagging. Before she knew it, she was love-forty down. She played the best she knew how, and recovered the next two points. Thirty-forty. She tried to ace Jessie-Ray to get even.

"Fault!"

The ball had been fractionally out. *I can't let this woman beat me again*, Kelly told herself. She risked going all out on the second serve, delivering a perfect ace to even the score.

"Fault!"

"What?"

Kelly couldn't believe it. She was so sure that the

ball had been in. The umpire shook his head. The crowd murmured. They weren't on Kelly's side.

"Fault. Game, Mrs Connor. Mrs Connor leads, five games to three."

Kelly went back to receive serve, reeling with disbelief. Two minutes ago, she had been on the verge of a break. Then a double fault cost her her own serve. Now she had to break serve to stay in the set. Before she knew it, she was thirty-love down. She fought back, evening the score, but then Jessie-Ray played a brilliant cross-court volley which Kelly couldn't read or reach. The crowd applauded wildly. *They love her*, Kelly realized. *Not me*.

"Forty-thirty."

Kelly gritted her teeth, knowing what was coming next. The best players could come up with a perfect ace when they needed one. Sure enough, the ball shot into the far right corner of the court. Kelly went for it full stretch, pelting the ball straight down the line. Jessie-Ray ran for it, but had no chance.

"Out!"

Kelly felt like crying.

"Game and first set, Mrs Connor, six games to three."

There was loud applause. *If they only knew*, Kelly thought. *If they only knew what she's done*. But luck wasn't on her side this afternoon. She sat down, sipped orange juice from a cardboard Coca-Cola cup, then hid her head in a towel. She wasn't ready to roll over and give up, that was for sure. If she was going to beat Jessie-Ray, she would have to make her own luck.

At least she was serving first in the second set. That was some kind of advantage. Kelly really had to fight now. She couldn't afford to go behind. But Jessie-Ray wouldn't let her get ahead either. The games went with serve, neither woman so much as getting a break point. It was the tightest, most competitive game that Kelly had ever played. She had to admire her opponent. Kelly was playing her best ever tennis, but it still wasn't good enough. She played every shot she knew, calculating the percentages the best she could. If she kept Jessie-Ray running, her opponent was bound to tire, start making mistakes.

At 6-5, Kelly got her chance. Jessie-Ray double faulted the opening point and muffed an easy return at thirty-all. Kelly had set point. She tried to concentrate. Instead, she heard voices in her head. She could imagine the TV commentator saying: "That isn't tennis out there, it's war." She could hear Mary saying "Concentrate, just concentrate." Jessie-Ray was in no hurry to serve. Then she did.

"Deuce."

The serve had rocketed past her, so fast Kelly didn't even try for it. The next one she put into the net. The one after that she put out.

"Six games all, second set. Tie-break."

In a tie-break, anything could happen. *Blink, and it's all over. Snap out of it*, Kelly told herself. *Lose this and you've lost the match*. She could feel the crowd urging the older woman on. They were all pulling for the sinner who'd been saved. Kelly served.

"One-love, Miss Christian."

Polite applause. They changed ends. Then Connor aced her. Loud cheers. Kelly couldn't remember playing a game with such ferocious support for her opponent before. She remembered what Mary told her: "For you or against you, you've got to learn to block the crowd out." She thought of Louise and how she might never play tennis again. She had to win for her. Jessie-Ray's next serve went out and the second service was short. Kelly ran forward, playing a stop volley that took all the pace off the ball; it drifted over the net. Incredibly, Jessie-Ray got it back. But she left Kelly with an easy lob. She was one break of service ahead.

"Two-one, Miss Christian."

Kelly held her next two serves. The crowd were quieter now; but it didn't matter either way, because Kelly was focused. Jessie-Ray must have been just a little bit rattled, but her next serve was a killer: a copy of the one which won her the first set. This time, though, Kelly connected perfectly. She volleyed the ball straight down the line. Jessie-Ray got to it, but sent the ball hopelessly into the crowd.

"Five-one, Miss Christian."

Jessie-Ray won her next serve, but it left Kelly only having to hold her own service points to win the set. In the first, she came out on top of a long rally. She had five set points ahead of Jessie-Ray. She could hear Jessie-Ray muttering to herself beneath her breath. *This one's for Louise*, Kelly thought as she tried to put as much topspin on to her serve as she possibly could.

"Game and second set, Miss Christian. One set all."

Jessie-Ray hadn't even gone for it. The crowd applauded loudly, happy that they were going to get another set of exciting tennis. *I can do it*, Kelly told herself. *I can really do it*. But there was no tiebreak in the final set. She would have to break Jessie-Ray, and not be broken herself.

The day was hot and getting hotter, but Kelly hardly noticed. When the third set began, everything went haywire. Jessie-Ray, furious at the way she'd lost the tie-break, came at Kelly's serve with everything she had. She won the first game with Kelly only taking two points. Kelly retaliated by lifting her play. In the second game, she broke Jessie-Ray for the first time, evening the score. Anything seemed possible now. Both women were drenched in sweat. They ran all over the court, going for impossible shots and, sometimes – to wild applause – getting them.

As the game wore on, each player's serves became less consistent, as did the score. But neither woman edged more than a game ahead. "You have to live in the moment," Mary always advised Kelly. "Take the match a point at a time." Now Kelly was forced to do that. She was totally concentrated, but couldn't get the match won. The crowd were going crazy, but Kelly hardly noticed, as the score grew higher and higher: 5-4, 5-5, 5-6, 6-6, 7-6, 7-7 and on and on...

Sweat streamed down Kelly's back. She could see that her opponent was tired. Now and then she could make out Andrew's voice in the excited crowd, urging her on. She had served for the match once, at 6-5, but Jessie-Ray had broken her. Jessie-Ray had served for the match at 7-6, but Kelly had broken her too. Now it was nine games all. Kelly could feel the muscles in her leg beginning to tighten. Soon, if she wasn't careful, she would get cramp. In the change-over, she did stretching exercises. Jessie-Ray stayed seated.

In the next game, Kelly made her serves as hard as she could, and Jessie-Ray pounded them back. Kelly stayed at the baseline, playing accurate per-centage tennis. Then, at thirty-fifteen, she came into the net, and won the point with a delicate drop volley. Forty-fifteen. But the next point, she double faulted. Forty-thirty. If ever she needed a big serve, now was the time. But her arms deserted her. The serve she struck was short and soft, even for a second serve. Jessie-Ray came in for it but, instead of capitalizing on the soft shot, was confused by it and hit the ball into the net. Game. Kelly had had a lucky escape. For the fourth time, Jessie-Ray had to serve to stay in the match.

Jessie-Ray wanted to serve straight away, but Kelly made her wait, making an imaginary adjustment to her socks, the way Mary had advised her to. All players used such gamesmanship, but Kelly didn't like doing it. She thought about tactics. Her opponent was tired. The sensible thing to do was play safe percentage tennis on the baseline and hope for a mistake. But Kelly decided to go for gold instead. She returned serve, then hurried into the net to reply with a half-volley. When Jessie-Ray lobbed her on the second point, Kelly ran around the ball and hit a cross-court volley. Jessie-Ray tried to reach it, but fell over instead.

Jessie-Ray got up. She looked awkward on her feet. Kelly had to get her *now*, while she was vulnerable. Jessie-Ray's next serve was a fault and the second service was a doddle. Kelly smashed it into the left-hand corner of the court.

"Love-forty."

Now the crowd were applauding Kelly. She had three match points. But she wasn't going to need three. *You got rid of Louise*, Kelly thought as she waited for the serve. *But I won't let you get rid of me.*

Jessie-Ray's serve thundered into Kelly's backhand. She returned it high. Jessie-Ray smashed it to the right of the court. Kelly sliced the ball back as Jessie-Ray hurried to the net and played a drop shot. Somehow, Kelly managed to dive for the ball and get beneath it, lobbing the ball high over Jessie-Ray's head. Her opponent smashed the ball back.

"Out."

Dimly, beneath the crowd noise, Kelly heard the umpire saying "Game, set and match, Miss Christian." She looked round to find Mary's and Andrew's faces in the crowd. They were standing, cheering, waving. Kelly was supposed to celebrate but she wasn't quite sure how. Mary was gesturing at her and Kelly suddenly realized what she was telling her to do. She ran up to the net and shook Jessie-Ray's hand. Neither of them smiled.

"I'll get you next time," Jessie-Ray grunted beneath gritted teeth. "Believe it."

Kelly found herself shaking the umpire's hand. Then she was receiving her cup, and the cheque. Kelly kept reminding herself to smile. It was like a dream. Indeed, she was convinced that it was still a dream when she walked into the locker-room to see Jessie-Ray being confronted by Detective Inspector Goad.

"Mrs Connor? When you've finished changing, I'd be grateful if you'd accompany me to the station. There are a few questions we'd like to ask you."

3

WIMBLEDON

15

Louise had been flown home. Andrew had returned to Scotland to take his final A-level. Kelly and Mary were alone in London, practising in Aorangi Park, next to the All England Tennis and Croquet Club in Wimbledon. Kelly had no idea what croquet was. Two courts away, Kelly could see Jessie-Ray, playing with Lacy Cannon, her doubles partner. Jessie-Ray had her hair tied back with a leather band, instead of the bandanna she wore for matches. It made her face look younger and more vulnerable. Lacy was laughing at a joke her fellow American had told her. Kelly winced. She could use a friend her own age now. But Lacy's new friendship with Jessie-Ray ruled out Kelly spending time with her. There was only Mary. She wished that

Andrew were here. Even more, she wished that François hadn't deserted her in Paris.

"Stop looking over there and serve."

Kelly still found it hard to beat Mary sometimes. Many people said that Mary had retired too early. After all, Navratilova reached a Wimbledon final when she was older than Mary was now. In the years since retiring, Mary had lost some of her speed, but none of her shots. She was passing them on to Kelly.

At least Kelly didn't have to qualify. And East-bourne had acclimatized her. People talked about how lousy the English weather was, how rain kept interrupting play. Yet today it felt more like Florida. Kelly wore sunscreen and moisturizer. She was only seventeen, but she had to protect herself against spots and wrinkling. Dry skin wouldn't look good in the ads she was about to do.

"That's enough."

Kelly followed Mary off court, glancing one more time at Jessie-Ray and Lacy. Both women were watched by their bodyguards. Kelly worried. Suppose Jessie-Ray *was* responsible for the attacks? Now Kelly had beaten her at Eastbourne, the older woman was bound to want Kelly out of the way. Kelly had to take care that what happened to Louise and Maria didn't happen to her. On court, Lacy waved at Kelly as she walked by. Kelly waved back. Jessie-Ray didn't turn round.

* * *

Mary and Kelly went to Knightsbridge where Kelly had a final fitting for her new image. Clothing for Wimbledon had to be predominantly white, but Kelly's top was spattered with insignias for the products she found herself promoting. The top was designed by Tula, the Italian sportswear manufacturers whose clothes Kelly had agreed to wear. Mary was on at her to go for a racket endorsement too.

"I'm not going to change rackets just before a big tournament," Kelly said.

"You don't have to change rackets," Mary explained. "Just the labels on the ones you use. The important thing is that you carry your rackets in the manufacturer's bag."

"But that would be lying."

"No. That would be business."

Kelly signed the contract. Then she went to have her hair done at Vidal Sassoon. She spent the afternoon having her photograph taken, finishing with more practice at Aorangi Park in the evening. Before going to bed, she rang Andrew to make sure he'd got home safely.

"I miss having you around," she said.

"Did you decide what to do about Kong and his offer of a bodyguard?" Andrew asked after a while.

"I'm still undecided. I don't want to feel obligated to Kong. I just don't know. I mean, Louise doesn't like him but she seems to trust him. For a while I suspected Kong of pushing her off the cliff. But he has no motive. What do you think?"

"I think you might be in danger of some kind," Andrew told her, "but I wouldn't take a bodyguard from Kong. Not if you don't trust him. I'll be there at the weekend. Until then, be careful."

His voice was more like that of a boyfriend than a hitting partner. They said good night tenderly.

The way Kelly had been playing the previous week, she thought she couldn't go wrong. But her over-confidence cost her. The next day, she lost the first set of her first match to a German qualifier. Then she was two points down in the second set tie-break before turning the game around. This near miss woke her up, and she won the final set 6-1.

"You don't want to peak too early," Mary told her afterwards. "But if I catch you playing so casually again, you'll have to find yourself a new coach."

Mary was right. Despite her lesson in Paris, Kelly had let herself be distracted. Moments before going on court, she'd been signing autographs and checking her new, carefully styled hair-do. She'd nearly made an expensive mistake. But it was partly Mary's fault, too. She was pressing Kelly to take on endorsements, to look glamorous. Mary got a per-centage of every fee. And now she wanted Kelly to do a short interview with the BBC.

"I'm not ready. I'm sure I'll make a fool of myself."

Kelly's previous interviews had been limited to short questions and answers after winning at Eastbourne and reaching the third round in France.

"They want to do a ten-minute profile, Kelly. It's great publicity. Just be yourself. There won't be any difficult questions."

"All right. But let me get through the next round first."

Kelly prepared hard for her second game. Her opponent was Lucia Almodovar. The Spanish player had been ranked higher than Kelly until she won at Eastbourne. At Wimbledon, though, Kelly blew her off the court, 6-1, 6-0. The small crowd on number fourteen court applauded enthusiastically.

"That was better," Mary told Kelly. "But you're having it too easy. I've arranged for someone to test you a bit more tonight."

Kelly turned up at Aorangi Park to find that her hitting partner was Ivan Matusec, the world number five. Mary had known him since he was a junior. Ivan had one of the most powerful serves in the game. He returned Kelly's serves as though they were made of putty. Kelly felt out of her depth and played badly. She wasn't helped by a constant, vague feeling that she was being watched, from a distance. It was probably only a fan, though, and she didn't mention it.

"It's too hard," she told Mary after fifteen minutes. "I'm not getting anywhere. I feel intimidated."

"This is only practice," her coach reminded her. "One day, you'll find yourself playing Sue Murray on Centre Court. Then you'll know what it's like to feel intimidated."

Matusec spoke little English and nodded curtly when Kelly thanked him for his help. Then he went off for some serious practice with his own hitting partner. Mary stayed on court with Kelly until dusk, going over the weak points in her game. Sometimes Kelly thought that Mary was making up weak points where they didn't really exist. Her coach was a perfectionist.

'Who do I meet in the third round?" she asked on the way to the hotel.

She and Mary had been due to rent part of a house in Wimbledon but had switched to a hotel because it had better security. If Kelly couldn't afford a bodyguard she could at least afford to feel safe in her room at night.

"No one difficult," Mary told her.

"Who?"

"Elaine."

Kelly groaned. She was fairly sure Elaine wasn't the one behind the mysterious "accidents". This was a good thing, because Elaine was staying in the same hotel as Kelly. That morning, she'd risked a smile at Elaine, but the South African girl ignored her. Kelly didn't like falling out with people. She'd snubbed Elaine in Eastbourne because of her suspicions about Edgbaston and the motorbike attack. Now that these seemed false, she wanted to make it up. But any reconciliation would have to wait until after their match.

"Show her no mercy," Mary told Kelly. "Do what you did to her at Eastbourne. She'll be trying to do the same to you."

16

Lacy Cannon won her third-round game easily. In the changing-room, Elaine Murdoch ignored Lacy as she came in from the court. Kelly congratulated her.

"Good luck," Lacy said, beaming. "And be warned, it's hot out there!"

But the heat was the least of Kelly's worries. This was a grudge match, but she wasn't in the mood for it. Kelly was sure that she had the measure of Elaine, but she wanted this match over as quickly as possible.

Elaine won the toss and elected for Kelly to serve. This suited Kelly fine. Her serve wasn't as strong as that of Lacy, who regularly topped a hundred miles an hour, but she was getting closer all the time. The practice with Matusec had made her feel tougher.

However, she wasn't warmed up yet, and her first serve was fractionally out. Her second serve was short and Elaine walloped it back. Kelly came in for it, allowing Elaine to catch her out with a passing shot.

"Love-fifteen."

Kelly lost the game and from there on nothing seemed to go right. Elaine played with a vigour and verve which Kelly had never seen in her before. Maybe this was how she'd won Edgbaston. Maybe food poisoning had nothing to do with it. Elaine was quickly 2-0 ahead. Everything she went for went in, while Kelly was barely holding half her serves.

They were thirty-all in the third game when Kelly double faulted for the first time, giving Elaine a break point. Kelly watched her enemy waiting for serve at the other side of the court. Elaine's body was twitching. She was pumped. Kelly took a deep breath, opened her shoulders, and served the biggest serve she knew how.

"Deuce!"

A perfect ace. Elaine thought it was out and complained to the umpire.

"There was chalk dust," she was told.

It wasn't over, though. Elaine had two more break points before Kelly wrested the game back from her. In the next game, Elaine won to love. She was 3-1 ahead. The crowd had stayed on from Lacy's match and court fourteen was nearly full. Neither girl was well-known, but they had won Edgbaston and Eastbourne between them. They had to be seen. Kelly held on to her next three serves. Even so, after half an hour on court, Elaine was serving for the first set, at 5-4. *I've got to break her*, Kelly told herself. But she had no idea how to do it.

The points passed quickly. Fifteen-love. Thirty-love. Thirty-fifteen. Forty-fifteen. Elaine had two set points. Kelly felt her blood was running cold. She tried to motivate herself to fight back. But all her thinking did was to show that, today, her concentration was off. Elaine rocketed another serve at her.

"Fault!"

Elaine grimaced and hit a strong second serve which skimmed the net.

"Let!"

The next ball landed just within the tramlines.

"Out!"

"Forty-thirty."

It was Elaine's first double fault. But it was still set point. Kelly had to take her chance. The next serve was more tentative. Kelly bashed it back, came into the net, then was forced to snatch at a clever cross-court volley from Elaine. She was sure that she was a goner. Yet, somehow, the ball trickled over the net and out of Elaine's reach.

"Deuce."

Kelly was still in the set thanks to luck, not skill.

But how she had survived made no difference. The tide had turned. Kelly slammed the next serve back, then caught Elaine out with a lob, gaining her first break point. It was the only one she needed. Elaine double faulted again. It was five games all. Kelly felt a bit more enthusiastic now. She seized the moment and won her serve game to love. The score was 6-5 in Kelly's favour. This was the time to break Elaine's serve and win the set, while she was still demoralized. But it didn't work out that way. Elaine started running more, forcing Kelly to do the same, and leaving her exhausted. Kelly got two points, but Elaine got two more.

"Six games all," the umpire called. "Tie-break."

Kelly started the tie-break with an ace. She needed to be perfectly concentrated now, to take every half chance. Elaine seemed to have put the double faults behind her. Each point was fiercely contested, and all but two went with serve. At 5-6, Kelly tried not to think about the fact that it was set point for Elaine. All she had to do was hold her serves and she would have set point herself. Kelly's first serve brushed the net and she had to take it again. This time, it went fractionally out. Her second serve had to be safer. She couldn't risk a double fault. Kelly served short. Elaine returned deep and Kelly only just managed to volley the ball back, coming into the net afterwards.

Kelly hoped Elaine would be forced into an error.

A weak return would allow Kelly to smash the ball safely out of reach. Instead, the South African also came into the net, and played a delicate drop shot. Kelly was forced to full stretch to get the ball, losing her balance as she did. The ball landed on the top of the net. As Kelly crashed to the ground, the ball seemed to hesitate on the net cord, deciding which way to fall. Then Kelly heard Elaine scream and realized that the ball had come down on her side. Elaine was reaching for it. Hurriedly, Kelly tried to get up, brushing the net. Elaine dived for the ball. Somehow, the two girls collided. Kelly was on the ground again, her side aching.

"Six points all."

Kelly tried to stand up. Had Elaine injured her deliberately? She looked over at the South African girl. Elaine was clutching her leg, appearing to be in pain. Was this some kind of ruse?

"Time out. Injury break."

Kelly walked over to her seat without looking back at Elaine. The South African girl must have tried to dive into Kelly and hurt herself instead. Served her right. Unless she was faking. In which case, it didn't matter. Kelly's side ached but she wasn't going to let this game get away from her. There was a rumbling, discontented groan from the crowd. Kelly saw that Elaine hadn't returned from the centre of the court. She was being examined by a doctor. The doctor stood and walked over to the umpire. The next thing Kelly knew, a stretcher was being brought on.

"Miss Murdoch is unable to continue," the Umpire announced. "Miss Christian wins the match by default."

Kelly watched as her rival was carried off. Then she packed her rackets and went over to shake the umpire's hand. The umpire ignored her. A few people in the crowd began to boo. *They think that I'm responsible*, Kelly realized.

"You could have gone over to see how she was," Mary told Kelly afterwards, as they walked over to the TV studio.

"She'd just tried to injure me!"

"You're getting too paranoid. That's not the way it looked from the stands. Two players crashed into each other. It doesn't happen often, but it's an occupational hazard. You ought to show sympathy. The crowd didn't like it."

The BBC made Kelly watch a video of the accident, then talk them through it. Mary was right. On TV, it looked like a 50:50 thing.

"How do you explain what happened?" the interviewer wanted to know.

"We were both going for impossible shots and getting them," Kelly said. "What happened could have happened to either of us. It was war out there."

"And how do you feel about the crowd booing you for your callousness?" Kelly wasn't sure what the word "callous" meant, but she got the idea.

"I know it looked like I wasn't concerned about Elaine, but I'd just had a pretty nasty knock myself. I wasn't thinking straight and didn't fully comprehend what had happened. Naturally, I'm concerned about her."

The interviewer didn't look convinced. Kelly was glad to get away from the press. She returned to her hotel, ignoring the reporters standing just outside the lobby.

"Any comment on Elaine Murdoch's injury, Kelly?"

"Was it deliberate?"

"Is it true that you two hate each other because you fell out over a boy?"

"Keep them away from me, please," she said to the doorman as she went inside.

When she got to her room, the phone was ringing.

"Kelly? How are you?" Peter Kong's voice said. "That was quite a fall."

"A couple of bruises, that's all."

"I wanted to say, if you need any advice or help, I'm here for you."

"Thanks. I appreciate that."

Kelly was being polite, but Kong was the last person she wanted to speak to at the moment.

"I have good contacts in public relations," Kong purred. "More in the States than here. I'll see what I can do to stop ugly stories circulating."

"Thanks."

Kelly wasn't sure she wanted Kong doing anything for her, but she couldn't work out how to say "no" without seeming rude.

"I wondered," Kong continued, "whether you'd reconsidered my offer of a bodyguard."

"It's very kind of you," Kelly said hesitantly, "but I'm getting by all right as I am."

The millionaire's voice became colder.

"From what I hear, your hitting partner has gone back to Scotland and your coach spends more time on TV commentary than she does on you. A professional bodyguard could protect you from the press as well as from … people with violent intentions. I urge you to reconsider, Kelly."

"OK," Kelly said. "I'll think about it. Thanks again for the offer."

She put the phone down. Why was she holding out against Kong's help? She didn't like the way that he used his money to buy the friendship of young players. It wasn't fair. But life wasn't fair, as Mary kept reminding her. If she told her coach of Kong's offer, Mary would advise her to accept it. Confused, Kelly rang Louise. Her friend sounded drowsy.

"I'm sorry. Did I wake you up?"

"It's all right," Louise said. "I sleep all the time at the moment. It's good to hear your voice. How did you get on today?"

Kelly told her, then asked after Louise's health. She was recovering slowly. The painkillers kept her doped up. Then Kelly asked about Kong. It was a sensitive subject, but when Kelly explained her situation, Louise opened up.

"You know, there are stories about him – that his money really comes from the Mafia, or he murdered his parents – but Tetsuo assures me they're all rubbish. I felt uncomfortable taking his money to help my parents last year but, when it came down to it, I needed his help. There was nowhere else I could go. But you'll notice his help is selective. He chooses the most attractive players…" Louise laughed. "Except me, of course. But we're the same race. Maybe he thought that gave him a chance with me."

"Did he try anything?" Kelly asked.

"Only in a clumsy way. He backed down quickly. I think that he's actually rather shy and lonely. Tennis is the only thing which interests him."

"So what should I do?"

"It sounds to me like you need a bodyguard. If Peter's offering to help, let him."

"But what are the strings?"

"The only strings are that you have to be nice to him. But tennis is full of people you hate who you have to be nice to. What difference does one more make?"

"None, I guess."

But when Kelly put down the phone, she still wasn't convinced.

17

The morning's papers made depressing reading: "SMASH! YOUNG STAR TAKES A FALL; TENNIS TERROR TOLL RISES!" and, worst of all, "ELAINE ACCUSES KELLY: 'YOU DID IT ON PURPOSE!'" Several papers had a photograph, the angle of which made it look like Kelly was kicking Elaine. The captions told a similar story. "*Not a very Christian thing to do.*" They made Kelly feel sick.

"The BBC are holding back their profile of you," Mary said. "They'll show it if you make it through the quarter-finals."

"Fat chance of that," Kelly said. "Who am I playing?"

"Lacy Cannon."

This made Kelly even more depressed. Why did she have to meet Lacy again?

"You beat her easily in Paris," Mary encouraged her.

"Yes, but she wasn't serving well then."

"I'll see if Matusec's free tomorrow," Mary said.

"I'll be quite happy practising with Andrew when he turns up later on," Kelly said. "I can't wait to see him."

"Ah…" Mary said.

"What's wrong?"

"Andrew rang while you were still asleep. He can't come till tomorrow. There's a big end of exams celebration tonight. All of his friends will be there and it might be his last chance to see some of them before they go off for the summer. He thought you'd understand."

"Of course," Kelly said, though it hurt her to remember that other people had a life. She had all but lost touch with her old friends at home.

"So let me call Matusec," Mary suggested again.

"No, it's all right, really," Kelly replied. "He's done us enough favours. I'll go down to the practice courts, find someone to hit with there. No problem."

She walked over to the courts. It was another brilliant, sunny day. Even the silly stories in the paper couldn't get Kelly down now. Of course

Elaine would say something like that: she was a bad loser, a spoiled brat. Sometimes, Kelly worried that she was becoming like her. Maybe that was the price of success. But it hadn't affected Lacy that way. Kelly knew that Lacy was good. Still, Kelly had beaten her before. So she could beat her again. She had to.

When she got to the courts, Kelly's mood changed abruptly. At first she thought it was her imagination. No one acknowledged her presence. Every time she tried to wave or nod at another player, she was blanked. Only Lacy gave her half a smile. Jessie-Ray, her hitting partner, ignored Kelly completely.

Mary had warned Kelly how this sort of thing happened on the tour. It was like the bullying which went on amongst twelve-year-old girls. No one called names. There was nothing physical. But you were excluded from the group's friendship, from the only circle that meant anything to you. It could be the most painful bullying of all. Was it because of what happened to Elaine, Kelly wondered, or did the other players suspect her of something worse? There was an unspoken hint in the papers that morning. Reading between the lines, the question was: *If Kelly could do something like that on court, what was she capable of off court?*

Kelly walked away. There was no way that she was going to find a hitting partner here today. As she got to the gate, she bumped into someone. Without looking at him, she mumbled an apology and hurried by.

"Hey!"

Kelly kept walking. It was probably someone who wanted to complain about the match yesterday. But then she recognized the voice.

"Kelly, it's me."

She turned round. A well-built, curly-haired young man held out his hand.

"We meet again."

Kelly had never felt so relieved to see someone in her life. She ignored his hand and kissed both his cheeks, in the French style.

"It's good to see you again, François."

"It's good to see you, too. I've had trouble tracking you down."

"Why are you here?"

"To play, of course. I'm into the second round of the Under-18s. But you don't follow Junior tennis, do you?"

Kelly apologized.

"I wish I'd been able to see you play at the French Open. How did you do?"

"You don't know?"

"I wouldn't be asking, would I?" she said.

François shrugged.

"I guess … anyway, I won it."

"You won? That's brilliant."

He gave a modest smile.

"I thought maybe you wanted a hitting partner."

"Yes, please."

Kelly found a free court and began to practise with her handsome Frenchman. The English hated the French, didn't they? Good, because she hated the English, especially their tabloid press and their snooty tennis clubs. She'd show them.

"We meet again," a cool American voice said.

François gave Mary a casual nod.

"I wasn't sure if you'd have a partner," Kelly's coach said, "so I came down. Ready for some tuition?"

"You bet," Kelly said.

Mary gave François a frosty look. *She thinks he's going to put me off my game*, Kelly thought. But she's wrong. François, Kelly realized as they started in earnest, was a better player than Andrew. His serves were stronger, and he had a much greater variety of strokes. He tested her more. Andrew was unable to play in the Juniors this year because of his exams. But if he were there, François would thrash him. Kelly knew that she still had feelings for the Frenchman. But, presumably, François didn't think of her romantically. Otherwise, he wouldn't have disappeared the way he did in Paris. Would he?

"What are you doing this weekend?" François asked when they'd finished. Kelly didn't know how to reply. She didn't know when Andrew was arriving, or how to tell François about him. Embarrassed, she glanced over at Mary.

"Kelly has a heavy practice schedule," Mary told him coldly. "Matusec is helping her with return of serve. And she has a new hitting partner arriving."

"Oh." François didn't look too pleased.

"Maybe we could meet up tomorrow … for lunch or something," Kelly half pleaded.

If Andrew had been at a party in Scotland the night before, he was hardly likely to arrive by lunchtime. Scotland was a long way away.

"Sure," François said. "But I was kind of hoping you could show me around. This is my first time in London. I'd like to see the West End."

"Then how about tonight?" Kelly suggested. "Saturday night's usually when a place is at its liveliest. There's no play tomorrow, so I can stay out late." Mary frowned, but the couple arranged to meet.

"What have you got against François?" Kelly asked her coach when the young Frenchman had left.

"Nothing," Mary said. "Except maybe his timing. You don't need distractions at the moment. Things are difficult enough."

Kelly lost her cool.

"I think his timing's excellent. In case you hadn't noticed, I really need a friend at the moment. You're doing so much TV commentary that I see you less and less. And, earlier on, nearly all of the other players blanked me. Do you know how that feels?"

"Oh, yes," Mary said. "I know how that feels. And I'll tell you something for nothing. The more successful you get, the more often it'll happen. And the harder it'll be to tell who are your true friends, rather than the false friends hanging on to you because of your money and fame. Don't let us fall out, Kelly. We've been together too long. I hope that François is good for you. Really I do. But be wary. And remember, Andrew's coming tomorrow. How are you going to explain François to him?"

"There's nothing between me and Andrew," Kelly insisted.

"I thought not," Mary said. "But is that what Andrew thinks?"

Kelly was silent.

"I'd better go," Mary said in a somewhat sulky voice. "See if I can find someone who'd like to go and see the new Andrew Lloyd Webber with me."

As her coach left, Kelly realized that the evening at the theatre was meant to have been a treat for her.

"Hey, wait!" Kelly called.

She caught Mary up.

"I don't want to fight with you over some boy," she said with an apologetic smile. "You're right. We've been together too long to argue."

Mary smiled ruefully.

"No. The reason we're starting to argue is precisely because we've been together so long. It's right that you should become more independent. Maybe I'm too cynical about men, in particular, but I've had some bad experiences. Use them because otherwise they'll use you, that's my motto."

"You talk about men the same way you talk about tennis."

"Bitter lessons, Kelly. Bitter lessons."

Mary rarely talked about her love life and Kelly didn't like to ask too much. Sometimes, it was better to let people reveal things when they were ready. They were approaching the hotel. Kelly wondered if Mary would be able to line herself up with a date tonight. Maybe there was something between her and Matusec. They crossed the quiet road as a familiar droning noise suddenly grew louder.

"Kelly, look out!"

Kelly glanced round. A grey motorbike was accelerating towards her, at speed. For a moment, she froze, not knowing which way to jump. It was the one – the same one as in Eastbourne. She'd dismissed that as a coincidence, an accident, but she'd been wrong. Someone really did mean to kill her.

"Kelly!"

Kelly jumped at the same moment as Mary dragged her out of the path of the motorbike. Its noise was deafening. She felt the heat from its engine as the speeding vehicle brushed her body. She and Mary landed in an undignified heap on the road.

"Thanks," said Kelly. "You saved my life."

"I doubt it," Mary said. "But you took your time getting out of the way."

"I … I froze," Kelly told her.

She looked around. There were no witnesses on the street.

"Maybe someone inside the hotel saw it," Mary said. "Did you notice the number-plate?"

Kelly shook her head.

"You were staring at it so hard I thought…"

Kelly began to cry.

"Who would want to do this?" she pleaded. "To me, and Louise, and Sue and Maria. Why?"

"I don't know," Mary told her. "A madman, I suppose. Let's get inside and call the police."

Inside the hotel, no one had seen the incident. Mary rang the police, then they sat in Kelly's room. They didn't have long to wait.

"Hello again," Kelly said to Inspector Goad.

The inspector explained that she was heading a special investigations unit, based at the All England Club, which was looking into the attacks on players.

"Have there been any others since Louise?" Mary asked.

"Not attacks, no, until this. There have been death threats, but those are probably the usual cranks stirred up by the recent publicity. Now, I want you to tell me in as much detail as possible about the motorbike which tried to run you over."

Kelly did as she was asked and Mary filled in some more details. But the information they had to give was woefully thin.

"The height of the driver, build, anything like that?"

Both shook their heads.

"Did you get any impression, from the posture perhaps, as to the sex of the rider."

"I assumed it was a man," Kelly said. "But I can't think of a reason why."

The inspector looked at Mary.

"I had the opposite feeling," Mary told her. "I thought the rider was a woman, but I can't put my finger on the reason. Intuition, maybe."

The inspector frowned.

"Now tell me more about this earlier attack, in Eastbourne."

"At the time I wasn't sure that it was an attack," Kelly told her. "Or I would have reported it."

She gave the inspector all the details, but there weren't many of them.

"And there weren't any witnesses to this incident either? Who did you tell about it?"

"Mary. This guy called Andrew who's my hitting partner. That's all."

"I see. He was the boy who helped you look around the hotel rooms in Eastbourne, was he?"

"Er, yes. Louise told you about that, did she?"

"Yes. She explained how you tracked down the perfume Baudelaire which her attacker was wearing. However, the person you suspected, Mrs Connor, had an impeccable alibi for the time of the attack."

"I see."

The inspector got up to go.

"I'll let you know if we get any more information about this incident, Miss Christian. Good luck in the rest of the tournament."

Then she paused at the door.

"Oh, by the way. Were either of you two interviewed about the death of Maria Hernandez?"

"No," Kelly said.

"Where were you when it happened?"

"Kelly was with me," Mary told the inspector. "We left our hotel together and were in a taxi cab nearby when Maria had her accident, or whatever it was."

When the inspector had gone, Kelly called Peter Kong.

"I don't know if you've heard," she said to the millionaire, "but I've been attacked again. I wonder if your offer of a bodyguard still stands?"

"Of course," Kong said. "I'm glad you've seen sense. I'll call the agency. Would you like me to get someone to you tonight?"

"The morning will be fine," Kelly said.

She didn't want anyone else around spoiling her romantic evening.

"Are you sure that was wise?" Mary asked, when Kelly finished talking to Kong. "I wish you'd discussed it with me first."

"What choice do I have?" Kelly retorted. "I need protecting. Have you got something against Kong?"

"Not personally, no," Mary said. "I've not had much contact with him. He arrived on the scene a short while before I retired. The more senior players wouldn't have much to do with him then, but he bought his way into the favours of some of the younger ones. There are all kinds of stories about him."

"None of them substantiated," Kelly argued.

"And none of them disproved, as far as I know," Mary replied.

They left the subject there.

Two hours later, Kelly and François were eating in the basement of a tiny, cramped Italian restaurant called Pollo, close to the West End. One of the other juniors had recommended it to François because it was cheap. Kelly had offered to pay for somewhere plusher, but François refused. She was glad he had. Leaving the hotel, she had been pursued by reporters. Somehow, they seemed to have more privacy in this crowded place where the food was simple but good.

Kelly told François the full story of what had happened to her since losing in the third round of the French Open. The only part of the story she missed out was Andrew and her sort-of-relationship with him. She implied that she had sneaked into Jessie-Ray and Elaine's bedrooms in Eastbourne without any help. The young Frenchman was silent for a long time. They finished their wine.

"I don't think you have strong enough grounds for suspecting Elaine," François said eventually. "Why would she try to murder both Hernandez and Chung? She wasn't due to play either of them. And there was no perfume in her room – it seems to me that Jessie-Ray Connor is a much stronger suspect."

"I guess you're right," Kelly said. "But she has an alibi for the attack on Louise. And why would she have had me attacked this afternoon? I can't play her before the semi-finals."

François shrugged.

"Revenge maybe, for beating her at Eastbourne. Perhaps she was sure you'd get through – it would look a lot more suspicious if you were attacked the night before you played her, wouldn't it? Though there is another possibility…"

"Who?"

"Lacy Cannon. You beat her too. You said she's the only girl apart from Louise who's been nice to you. Maybe she's covering the fact that she's responsible."

Kelly shook her head.

"I like Lacy. That explanation's too paranoid for me."

She smiled reassuringly and moved the conversation on to pleasanter things.

19

Kelly woke early, thinking about the evening she'd spent with François. He had been the perfect gentleman, seeing her to the door and politely refusing her invitation to come in. But there had been nothing polite about their good night kiss. The couple hadn't made a date to meet again, but did exchange phone numbers. And François had made his intentions crystal clear last night. Kelly knew how she felt, too. She'd known since their first day together at the French Open.

Maybe François was unreliable. He had failed to explain why he dropped her in Paris and Kelly hadn't asked him. She was willing to let bygones be bygones. François treated her like an equal. That was important. Despite having won a championship, he was modest about his tennis. She liked that in him. Andrew, on the other hand, was confident about his abilities, and seemed confident that he could get off with Kelly if he made a move for her. Last year, maybe, she would have fallen for him. But she'd grown up a lot since last year.

How could she tell Andrew all of this tomorrow? Did she have to tell him anything? All they'd really had, this year and last, was a mild flirtation. Even so, Andrew might think that she'd been using him. To some extent, he'd be right. Kelly didn't want to hurt Andrew. She would have to pick her moment, let him down gently. But what about François? As soon as he was knocked out of the boys' tournament, he'd be gone. Kelly would be alone again. Could she bear that? Not with all the other things going on in her life at the moment.

There was a knock on her door. Kelly pulled on a dressing-gown and opened it. A heavy-set giant of a man with Nordic features stood there.

"I'm Olav. Mr Kong sent me. I have the room next door."

"All right," Kelly said. "Give me a minute to get dressed and I'll join you there."

When she'd briefed Olav about her movements, Kelly went down for an early breakfast. To her surprise, Lacy joined her. Her bodyguard and Lacy's stood near the entrance to the restaurant, like Tweedledee and Tweedledum, watching them.

169

"There was something I wanted to say," she told Kelly.

"Yes?"

"After my game on Saturday I had a shower and came out to watch you and Elaine."

"Checking out the competition, eh?"

"That's right. I had a really good view of the incident."

The incident. Kelly knew that "incident" was a euphemism for *scandal*.

"It was an accident," Lacy went on, in a sympathetic voice. "Neither of you meant it to happen. You could just as easily have been hurt as Elaine. If anyone asks me my opinion, I'll tell them that, too."

"Thanks," Kelly said. "I appreciate that."

They talked some more. Lacy questioned Kelly about Andrew, and about François, who she'd seen Kelly hitting with the day before. Kelly played her cards close to her chest. Lacy, after all, would say nothing about her own love life. The way she talked about sex, Kelly presumed that she had one. A short while later, Lacy got up to go.

"I'll see you on court tomorrow," she said. "May the best player win."

Kelly smiled.

"As long as it's me," she joked. "Nice having breakfast with you."

"And you."

When Lacy had gone, Mary came down. Kelly

asked her about the musical the night before. It was clear that she'd gone on her own. Kelly felt guilty.

"What were you doing just now?" Mary asked. "Softening up the opposition?"

"She came and sat with me."

"Then she was softening you up," Mary said. "I hope you didn't give anything away."

"There's nothing to give away," Kelly said.

Mary gave Kelly a lecture on tactics. Kelly barely listened. She hated it that she had to regard every conversation with another girl player as some kind of espionage. She hated that all anyone cared about was winning and it didn't matter how you did it. She hated herself and what she was turning into. As far as she could see, Lacy was a nice, genuine person. Kelly had had enough. She would train today, sure, but tomorrow, she would tank. She'd had enough of Wimbledon, enough of tennis. She wanted to go home.

20

"I miss you, Mom."

"You've been away too long, honey. Look, I promise, if you make it to the semis, your father and I will fly over. We'll get the time off work somehow."

"Thanks, but it isn't going to happen."

"Think positively, Kelly. How many times have you played Lacy. Five? Six?"

"Seven."

"And how many times has she beaten you?"

"Twice."

"That's right. And she hasn't beaten you once since you went pro. Think positively and you can win this. We love you, Kelly. We'll be rooting for you."

"I know. Thanks, Mom."

Kelly didn't have the heart to tell her mother the reason she was so fed up. If her mother had been here with her then yes, maybe she could have told her about François and the attacks and her growing disillusionment with the tour. But Kelly didn't want her parents watching at Wimbledon. Their presence always made her nervous. They wouldn't be coming to the semis, anyway. Tomorrow, she was going to lose.

"Here he is."

Andrew arrived just as Kelly was warming up at Aorangi Park.

"Sorry I'm a day late," he said warmly.

"It's all right," she told him. "I got by."

"Who's that?" he asked, pointing at the muscular Swede by the edge of the court.

"My bodyguard," she admitted. "I had to accept Kong's offer after what happened yesterday."

"What *did* happen yesterday?"

She told him. Soon, he was serving to her: big, easy serves, not much different from Lacy Cannon's, nowhere near as good as François's. Kelly played badly. She would have to tell him, later. She didn't know what words to use.

"What's got into you?" Andrew asked when they'd finished. "You haven't been taking notice of those stupid stories in the tabloids, have you?

Believe me, everybody in this country knows that they're nothing but lies."

"It's not that."

The four of them went back to the hotel. Kelly kept trying to find time to ring François, but Mary and Andrew didn't leave her alone for a moment. Olav stood discreetly by. They were concerned for her, she knew, but it was frustrating. During dinner, she got up to go to the toilet and slipped into the phone booth in the lobby. François's phone rang and rang, but there was no reply.

The next morning, Kelly checked the order of play and saw that François wasn't playing. She phoned his flat, only to be told that he had already gone out to practise.

"Tell him that Kelly called," she said. "Tell him I've been trying to reach him."

She would tell Andrew, she decided, before the match this afternoon. Then her head would be clear, unclouded by guilt, when she went on court. She still had no desire to win and felt terribly shaky. But she wanted to give a good account of herself. Representatives of her new sponsors would be there. She hoped, too, that François would be watching.

Her warm-up went well. She had a light packed lunch planned, and Andrew went with Mary to collect it from the car. Kelly sat on the soft grass, thinking about her match that afternoon. A hand squeezed her shoulder. She looked up, expecting to see Andrew. It was François.

"Where have you been?" he asked. "I kept ringing and going round to your hotel yesterday. I got nowhere."

"I tried to contact you," Kelly told him. "I missed you."

"It's all right," he said, holding her. "I'm here now."

They kissed – a long, passionate kiss this time, like two people in love.

"What do you think you're doing?"

François reeled round. Andrew's face was flushed red.

"Who the hell is this?" the young Scot asked.

Kelly stumbled for words. She hoped that Mary might explain, but her coach was a few yards behind Andrew. François turned to Kelly.

"What's going on?"

"I haven't had time to explain," Kelly said.

"I think, perhaps," François said to Andrew, "it would be best if you left us alone for a short while."

"Don't tell me what to do. You're the one messing with my girlfriend." As Andrew said this, François looked at Kelly, a sense of betrayal on his face. That was when Andrew hit him. The French boy turned round, winded, and Andrew grabbed him. Within a moment, they were wrestling on the floor.

"Stop it!" Mary shouted, hurrying up to them. "Can't you see that there are photographers around?"

Olav stepped forward, separating the two boys. Mary handed Kelly the car keys.

"Get in the car, out of sight."

"But I want to…"

"You've got a quarter-final to play. Do as you're told."

Kelly did as her coach suggested. François hurried away, while Mary stayed and talked to Andrew. Olav got into the car. Five minutes later Mary joined them.

"Let's go."

"What about them?"

"No damage done."

"Is François…"

"I don't want you talking about boys now," Mary interrupted. "I want you talking about Lacy Cannon."

21

The Cannon-Christian match was down to be played on Number One court, followed by Connor-Kieslowski. The other quarter-finals were on the legendary Centre Court, where Kelly had yet to play.

"You'll get to Centre Court on Thursday," Mary told Kelly as she went into the locker-room. Kelly didn't think so. Lacy would be playing Jessie-Ray Connor or Krystal Kieslowski in the semi-final, not her. But Lacy hadn't arrived yet. Kelly checked her watch: ten to two. They were meant to start warming up at two. Probably, Lacy had been waylaid by more autograph hunters. She'd better hurry.

At five to, Lacy came into the locker-room with her coach, Chuck. Chuck wasn't meant to be in there but Lacy was crying and Kelly said nothing.

"Could you give us a minute?" Chuck asked Kelly.

"Sure."

Kelly put on her Walkman, turned up the sound, then sat on the toilet. Lacy must be having some kind of crisis, but she wasn't going to eavesdrop. Let the girl have her privacy. She could have the match, too. Kelly hadn't told Mary, but she had already reserved her seat on a flight home. The plane left Heathrow at six, London time. By midnight, Massachusetts time, Kelly would be in bed, asleep.

It was two minutes to two when Kelly came out. Chuck was gone. Lacy was slipping on her tennis shoes. She ignored Kelly. These moments with the two of you alone in the locker-room before a game were never easy. The only worse times were when you had to get changed after a game with the player who'd just beaten you. There was a knock on the door and the tournament referee came in to wish them luck. Then the two young women went out to play.

As they knocked up, it began to dawn on Kelly: here they were, two seventeen-year-old girls, in a Wimbledon quarter-final. It wasn't a unique situation, but it was extremely unusual. No matter what had happened before, she had to give a convincing performance. It was a matter of pride, of honour. She looked up to the stands to smile at

Mary, then made the mistake of having a quick look around at the audience. There was Peter Kong, with his Cheshire-cat smile. There was a member of the British royal family. There was a famous film star. There was a rock musician whose picture she once had on her wall. It was overwhelming.

What followed was the most abysmal game of tennis Kelly had ever been involved in. She couldn't concentrate. She avoided looking towards Mary because she didn't want to see any of the crowd. This meant that she got no encouragement at all, because the crowd were all behind Lacy. They even applauded Kelly's mistakes. Her serve kept going out and her second serve was weaker than a twelve-year-old's. Her backhand went to pieces, and she completely forgot her game plan. In the first set, Kelly double faulted seven times.

The only thing was, Lacy played even worse. Kelly wanted to lose. But Lacy seemed incapable of winning. She kept missing the easiest of volleys. She stayed at the baseline when coming into the net would have paid huge dividends. Her serve was more like a beachball than a cannon-ball. When she did hit it hard, it nearly always went out.

Kelly won the first set, 6-2. In the change-over, early in the second set, she tried to work out what was happening. Maybe Lacy was freaked by the prospect of playing Jessie-Ray in the semis. After all, Jessie-Ray was her doubles partner. Or maybe there was some personal crisis in her life – a parent dying, something like that. What should Kelly do? It was no longer a matter of who wanted to win the most. It was who wanted to lose the least. To lose, Kelly would have to play so badly that she would severely damage her reputation. She couldn't do that. Her reputation was damaged enough already. She would have to play to win.

The next set took fifteen minutes, some kind of record. Kelly played better than in the first, but not much. Lacy won only seven points, most of them gifts from Kelly. The crowd's applause was lukewarm, but Kelly was through, 6-2, 6-0.

Lacy didn't go to her press conference, incurring a fine. Kelly unwound with a bath (Wimbledon was the only tournament which had baths), then braved the media. She admitted that she'd played badly in the first set, felt lucky to still be in the tournament and yes, maybe both players had felt over-awed at the prospect of playing in the semi-finals. Then she went out to watch the Connor-Kieslowski match, arriving in time for the end of the first set.

"What happened out there?" Mary asked when they were sitting together. "In the first set, it looked like both of you were tanking."

"The occasion got to me," Kelly explained. "It won't happen in the semis."

"What was wrong with Lacy?" Mary asked.

"I don't know," Kelly said. "Maybe the same

thing. I thought maybe I'd call her later. She seems really messed up."

"I wouldn't rub salt in her wounds if I were you."

"I guess."

They watched some of the next quarter-final. It was going with serve, but Jessie-Ray kept raising her game. The crowd, disappointed by the previous match, were getting behind both players. Jessie-Ray, with her bandanna and her expansive gestures, had the younger members of the crowd behind her. Kieslowski was a more delicate, elegant player. Mary watched intently. Doubtless she was remembering her last appearance at Wimbledon, when Jessie-Ray knocked her out in the semi-finals.

Now and then, Mary pointed out minor weaknesses in each player, but Kelly couldn't always see them. What she could see was that Krystal played intelligently. She treated the court like a chess board, calculating every move, trying to trick Jessie-Ray, to tire her.

If Jessie-Ray is the person behind it all, Kelly thought, *why hasn't something happened to Krystal?* Despite the Czech player's skill, Jessie-Ray's superior strength pulled her through on the tie-break, 8-6. The second set went the same way, with the American winning 12-10. It was the narrowest of victories: 7-6, 7-6. Kelly was glad that she had

Jessie-Ray, not Krystal, in the semi. She felt she had a better chance against her. Back in the hotel, she watched Jessie-Ray's TV interview after the match.

"How do you feel about facing Kelly Christian again?"

Connor smiled ruefully.

"I feel great about it. I want revenge for Eastbourne. I beat her in Paris, which was the important one. I'm sure I can beat her again."

"Will it be a good match? Her two-setter with Lacy Cannon today was … disappointing, to say the least."

"Both girls can play a lot better than they did this afternoon," Jessie-Ray insisted. "On Thursday, we'll see what Kelly Christian's made of."

Concerned about Lacy, Kelly decided to go and see her, no matter what Mary said. Lacy was still in the doubles with Jessie-Ray, so she wouldn't have gone home yet. Kelly considered ringing the room first, but decided against it. Lacy had told her what room she was staying in. She wouldn't mind if Kelly just stopped by.

"I'm not leaving the hotel," she told Olav when he got up to follow her. "There's no need for you to come."

Finding the room, Kelly knocked on the door.

"It's open," Lacy's voice yelled. "Bring the food in."

Kelly went into the room.

"Actually," she started to say, "it isn't room service, it's…"

But Lacy wasn't there. Kelly heard the shower being turned off. She called Lacy's name.

"What is it? Just leave the food and get out, please."

Kelly stood awkwardly by the dressing-table. She couldn't help seeing the perfume bottle in front of her, the top half inch empty: *Baudelaire*.

Kelly's head began to spin. Was Lacy the one who tried to have her run over yesterday? She tried to dismiss the suspicion from her mind. Lacy stepped out of the shower into the bedroom, a towel wrapped round her.

"What are you doing here?"

"I came to…"

"How dare you come into my room?"

"But…"

Kelly was embarrassed. Yesterday, Lacy had been so friendly. Today, she was full of rage. Someone else stepped out of the shower and walked into the bedroom.

"Hey, honey, what's…"

Lacy's coach stared at Kelly.

"How did you get in here?"

"I'm sorry, I…"

Kelly had heard plenty of stories about players having affairs with their coaches, but it had never occurred to her that Lacy…

"OK," Lacy raised her voice. "Now you know about Chuck and me. Big deal. Perhaps you want to tell your friend on the motorbike, the one who gave me this!"

She pulled the towel from round her shoulders to reveal a large, purple bruise which stretched down the top part of her right arm.

"Was he meant to break it?" Lacy asked, her voice rising, "or did you tell him to hit me just hard enough to ruin my game?"

"I had nothing to do with it!" Kelly insisted. "In fact, a motorcyclist tried to run me over, twice!"

"Oh, sure," Lacy said sarcastically. "I defended you when other girls said you were behind the attacks. Jessie-Ray warned me to be on my guard. I was *so* naive. But I'm not so naive that I believe this story about you being attacked too. You hurt the ones who are nicest to you, is that it? Me, Louise…"

"Lacy, that's ridiculous. You can't possibly believe…"

"You were there when Louise fell, weren't you? But I'll bet you have an alibi for the motorbike that ran into me this morning. Who did you pay, Kelly? How much did it cost?"

They were interrupted by a voice from behind the open door.

"Room service."

"Leave it on the floor outside," Lacy yelled. Then she addressed Kelly. "Get out of here," she said. "But first, tell me why you came in the first place. To gloat or to spy?"

"Never mind why I came," Kelly retorted. She was angry now. All hopes of friendship were shattered. "Just tell me one thing. How long have you been using that perfume?"

Lacy shook her head in disbelief at the absurdity of the question.

"It was a present from Jessie-Ray. What's got into you, Kelly? You used to be really nice. Even yesterday, I thought…"

"Leave it," Chuck said. "Get out of here, Kelly, or I'll call hotel security."

Kelly left, kicking over the couple's champagne and smoked salmon sandwiches as she walked down the corridor, trying to hold back tears.

22

"Where's Andrew?"

"He quit," Mary told Kelly. "What did you expect? An apology?"

"I guess not."

Kelly and Mary began to knock up.

"You don't need him anyway," Mary said. "We know Jessie-Ray's game inside out. Between us, we can work out how to beat her."

Kelly nodded. She had spent a lonely night the night before, thinking hard. She still suspected Jessie-Ray, rather than Lacy. After being questioned in Eastbourne, Jessie-Ray must have known that the perfume made her a suspect. Maybe that was why she'd given a bottle to Lacy, to cast suspicion elsewhere. Now that she was through, Kelly badly wanted to beat Jessie-Ray on Thursday.

"Concentrate!"

Kelly sleep-walked through the practice. There were two days before she had to play again. She could afford to ease into it. At least no one could accuse her of having peaked too early. She had played badly all the way through Wimbledon, yet she was still in the semi-finals. Sometimes, things worked out that way.

"Where are you going?" Mary asked as Kelly took off after lunch.

"To watch some tennis. I'll see you at the hotel later."

Olav and Kelly went to one of the smaller courts. Kelly's romance with François was in limbo until she got a chance to explain about Andrew. But she still wanted to see him play. She owed him that much. Today, he was in the third round of the Boys' tournament (the Junior tournaments got going later in the fortnight, as the number of matches in the Senior tournament lessened).

The audience in Court Ten was thin and became thinner when the match before François's finished. There was no British interest in his match. If François looked round, he was bound to see Kelly. But he was totally concentrated on his game. Kelly was amazed at how strong his matchplay was. He was really exciting to watch. She was sure that the Frenchman had a brilliant future in tennis, if he was willing to put his education on hold, the way she had hers.

François won 6-1, 6-1. Kelly joined in the warm applause at the end. The winner and his opponent shook hands with the umpire. Then, instead of leaving the court, François bounded over to Kelly.

"Like what you saw?"

The people standing around Kelly stared. Most of them hadn't noticed that one of the Ladies' semi-finalists was standing in the audience.

"Very much," she said. "How long have you known that I was there?"

"The players in the previous game told me. Us tennis bums rarely miss a pretty face, especially a famous one like yours."

Kelly smiled awkwardly. She didn't know whether François had come over to taunt her, or to make up with her.

"Give me five minutes," he said. "Wait here."

She did as she was told. Ten minutes later he was back, looking remarkably fresh for somebody who'd just played two sets of tennis.

"You raised my game," he told her. "I realized, as I was serving for the match, that I had to give you a third chance."

"A third?" Kelly queried. "I know what happened yesterday but, before that, as I recall, it was you who dropped me."

François looked hurt.

"You mean in Paris? But I tried … oh, never mind. I hear that there is this tradition at Wimbledon – strawberries and cream. You want to try it?"

"Only if you let me pay," Kelly said. "I hear they charge a lot for them." She bought two tiny bowls of strawberries and a glass of champagne each, too, to celebrate François's victory. They made small talk about their games.

"I saw you on TV," François said. "You were terrible."

"I'll tell you why some other time," Kelly said, draining her drink. The alcoholic bubbles gave her confidence. "First, I want to explain about Andrew." François grimaced.

"The young man who hit me yesterday?"

"That's the one."

"I'm – how do you say? – all ears."

Kelly did her best to tell the truth about Andrew without hurting François's feelings too much. She had been low after losing in Paris, she said, and thought that François had rejected her. Maybe she had led Andrew on, but nothing had happened. She'd needed some attention, that was all. It wasn't serious. When François returned, she knew she wanted him more. She'd been searching for the moment to tell Andrew.

"Instead I blundered by and kissed you, making him jealous," François said ruefully.

"Something like that."

"And nearly made you lose your match into the bargain."

"I had other things on my mind, too."

She glanced at Olav. François took her meaning and squeezed Kelly's hand.

Kelly didn't get back to the hotel until late.

"Where have you been?" Mary asked. "Your parents rang, twice. They're flying in tomorrow."

"No," Kelly protested. "I really didn't want them to come."

"Tough," Mary said. "You should have been here. And there have been loads of requests for press interviews. I've put them all off. Were there any journalists hanging around when you got in just now?"

Kelly shook her head. She'd been out with François again, celebrating his victory. He had walked her back to the hotel during a summer storm. She had worn an old, borrowed raincoat and a pair of ugly, clear plastic glasses which she'd picked up on the Tottenham Court Road. If there had been any press around, it must have proved a good disguise. Or maybe they were put off by Olav, walking a few paces behind. Either way, no one had approached her.

"Peter Kong rang too," Mary said. "He wanted to know how you were getting along."

"I guess it's too late to ring him back now," Kelly told her. "I'll do it in the morning."

Kelly wanted to tell Mary about her evening with François. Normally, she told Mary everything. Yet, tonight, her coach didn't seem curious. At times, Mary was like a mother to Kelly. At other times, a sister. Today, though, she was in professional mode. Maybe it was because Kelly's real family were flying in the following day.

Kelly had arranged to meet François at Aorangi Park the next morning. She told Mary but her coach wouldn't let her go out.

"There are too many press around," she said, "all baying for your blood."

"I'll disguise myself."

"That might work at night, but not in the day, Kelly."

Kelly rang François's flat, but he had already left. She didn't care what Mary said. Once her parents arrived that evening, she'd have even less time to see François. She wanted to see him now. Instead of going to lunch, she put on her frumpy plastic glasses, tied her hair back, and bribed one of the maids to lend her a spare uniform. Kelly didn't tell Olav where she was going. She hadn't found time to return his employer's phone call either. Kong could wait.

Kelly left the hotel by a back door and walked

right past the press pack in the front of the hotel. That was how she saw Lacy Cannon leaving.

"Why have you withdrawn from the doubles, Miss Cannon?" a reporter asked. Lacy shook her head and got into a taxi as cameras clicked. Before joining her in the car, Chuck spoke to the press pack.

"Lacy sustained an injury shortly before her match on Monday which she didn't have time to get treated. Her arm is fractured and the fracture was made worse by her playing two sets of strenuous tennis. Naturally, Lacy's upset about letting Mrs Connor down, forcing their withdrawal from the Ladies' doubles. But Jessie-Ray understands."

"Was the injury another criminal one, like the attacks on Louise Chung and Maria Hernandez?"

"You'll have to ask the police if they think it was an accident or an assault. We're not saying. Now, I'm sorry, but we have a plane to catch."

"What about Kelly Christian, Chuck? Could she have been responsible?" Lacy's lover got into the car without replying. Kelly left before any of the reporters noticed that she was listening. As she walked hurriedly on, Lacy's taxi drove past her, then slowed down. From the back seat, Lacy stared at Kelly, her face filled with recognition and hatred.

"What kept you?" François asked. "Why the absurd disguise?"

"I can't explain now," Kelly told him. "We have to practise some other place."

"But I have a game in two or three hours!"

"I know," Kelly said. "And I'm sorry, but I can't watch it. I have to meet my parents at the airport."

François shrugged.

"You can hardly play me wearing a maid's uniform."

"At least I've shaken off the press."

Kelly called Mary from François's flat. Her coach had managed to arrange a practice court at a private home, but there wasn't time for François to go there with her. When the car pulled up outside the flat, she offered him a lift to the All England Club. François refused.

"I think it's safest if we're seen together as little as possible. Otherwise we'll have these ... imbeciles from the tabloids camped outside my door, too."

Kelly met the plane at six. Even her brother had come for the semi-final. There was a joyful reunion at the airport. Kelly assured her mum and dad that she would be flying back with them, on Friday or Sunday. Whatever happened, Kelly decided, she was due some time off. She would rest up until the Virginia Slims tournament.

Only when she'd made this promise did Kelly remember that the final of the Boys' tournament wasn't until Sunday, after the Men's singles final. If

François got that far, she would have to leave later. That was it, then. She would have to beat Jessie-Ray and get to the final. She had to win.

23

Kelly slept better that night than she had done since arriving in England. Being with her family made her feel more secure, more human. They could talk over what was happening at home, share memories, stories and secrets. Her family were all worried about what they'd read in the American press concerning the dangers to female tennis players. Luckily, it seemed that Peter Kong had kept his promise about public relations. After the accident with Elaine, none of the US papers had attacked Kelly the way the British ones had. Kelly didn't tell her family much about François. That relationship was too new, too fragile, to be exposed to parental scrutiny. She arranged to see him, though, before her match. Spending time with him made her feel better about herself.

The phone rang in Kelly's room just as she was getting out of the shower. She nearly didn't answer it, worried that the caller might be from the press. Kelly was due to meet her family for breakfast in twenty minutes. She didn't want anything to put her in a bad mood.

But it wasn't the press. It was Louise, calling from Hong Kong.

"You don't know the trouble I've had getting a line," she said. "Then the hotel were really reluctant to put me through, in case you were sleeping. 'I know her,' I said. 'She hardly sleeps before a big match.'"

Kelly laughed. It was great to hear her friend's voice. She realized how isolated she'd become recently.

"I called to wish you good luck," Louise said. "I know you can beat Jessie-Ray again. You don't need me to tell you how. This time, you can go all the way to a Grand Slam final. Wouldn't it be great if we'd won one each?"

"I guess," Kelly said. "But I'm taking it one step at a time. How's your leg?"

"On the mend, as they say. I should be able to walk on it by August."

"That's great."

They talked for a while longer, then Louise lost the line. Kelly put the TV on as she dressed. The BBC were showing short profiles of the semi-finalists. The one on Jessie-Ray was just finishing:

"If she could win Wimbledon, the one Grand Slam title which eluded her as a sixteen-year-old, then her comeback would be completely vindicated.

"Ironically, her opponent today is a girl the same age as Jessie-Ray was when she 'retired' – and a girl who is rapidly becoming equally controversial."

The picture cut to images of the tussle which ended with Elaine leaving the match, injured. The crowd's boos and catcalls were amplified. Then the picture cut to a smiling Kelly. It was the interview she'd done the day before playing Elaine.

"I was born in Nahant, Massachusetts. Not many people know this, but my town hosted the first ever grass court tournament, back in the 1800s. So, when I come to Wimbledon – this is my second time – I kind of feel at home."

Then there was a montage of pictures of Kelly growing up, accompanied by a voice-over.

"Kelly's parents encouraged her to play from the age of four. By the time she was seven, Kelly was winning children's tournaments. At twelve, she was talked about as a future champion. Last year, at sixteen, she got to the quarter-finals of the Girls' tournament at Wimbledon and her parents finally allowed her to turn professional. This year, she's gone a stage further in the main tournament, without playing her best … yet."

There was an embarrassing bit with Kelly

burbling on about how exciting it had been to beat Jessie-Ray at Eastbourne and how Kelly felt she'd never played better.

"Do you think you could beat her again here, where it really matters?" Kelly shrugged and gave a girlish giggle.

"I can't meet her before the semi-finals. I don't think I'll get that far."

"But get that far she has," said the commentator, "to everybody's surprise, including mine. Yet Kelly's clean-cut, all-American image has taken a knock since her match against Elaine Murdoch. Kelly is an increasingly controversial figure. Today's broadsheets mention allegations of 'unfair interference' with Lacy Cannon before last Monday's quarterfinal. The tabloids, meanwhile, lead on gossip about Kelly's love life. We'll see whether the quality of her tennis can lift her above these squalid stories."

The report finished with images of Kelly beating Jessie-Ray at Eastbourne, but Kelly was no longer watching. She wanted to know what stories about her love life had appeared in the tabloids.

She didn't have long to wait. When she got down to breakfast, late, her mum, dad and Kevin had the morning papers spread out in front of them. The *Sun* was the worst:

"Jilted! Kelly Christian's boyfriend tells of how she two-timed him with a mysterious French lover."

Kelly groaned. The paper had an exclusive

interview with Andrew. He'd given them some photos taken the year before. The story implied that he and Kelly had a serious, long-term relationship until the "mysterious Frenchman" came along.

"I don't think you ought to read it," her mother said. "I'm sure it's all lies." But there was enough truth in the report to hurt Kelly. She couldn't believe that Andrew had invented so much lurid nonsense. "We were deeply in love," he'd written. Across the table from her family, Kelly's face turned bright red.

"Show me the others," she said.

The *Daily Mirror* also had the story about Kelly and Andrew. They had François's name, too. The broadsheet *Guardian* reported that police were investigating allegations of foul play before Kelly's match with Lacy.

"It's all nonsense," Dad told her. "We're with you a hundred per cent."

"I'm worried," Mum told them all. "The papers are stirring up so much hatred for Kelly. Suppose someone attacks her. Remember what happened to Monica Seles in the early nineties?"

"Security's a lot tighter since then," Kelly said.

But that hadn't helped Louise, or Maria.

"Here," said her brother Kevin. "Take this."

He produced a small canister from his pocket.

"What is it?" Kelly asked.

"It's a new kind of anti-mugging device. It works

like a miniature cattle prodder. You activate it with this button at the side. Anyone who touches the end gets a strong electric shock. Mom bought it to protect me against muggers on the way to school."

"You shouldn't have brought it on the plane," Dad said. "I don't even know if they're legal in this country."

"I brought it to protect Kelly," Kevin said.

"Thanks," Kelly told him. "I appreciate your thinking of my safety."

She put the canister in her bag and forgot about it.

The security around Centre Court was intense. Kelly was only able to snatch a few private moments with François outside the locker-room.

"Those stories in the press are nonsense," he said. "No one believes those comics."

"I told you the whole truth about Andrew," she said. "You know, I've never..."

"It's OK," he said, putting a finger to her lips in case anyone was listening. "I believe you. I believe in you. Put the papers behind you. Today is your day. You can do it."

They kissed before Mary came along and interrupted them.

"You're on your own now," Mary said, as she left Kelly. "Believe in yourself. You can go all the way."

Kelly went into the locker-room.

Jessie-Ray was already there, head in hands, concentrating – or meditating – the way she had done during the break in the French Open. That match was only four weeks ago, but it seemed like a lifetime. The older woman looked vulnerable and tired. If she wasn't the guilty one, then she must have been going through the same tensions as Kelly. If. Kelly had no idea who was guilty of what any more. When she started to think about it, her head began to spin. If someone really wanted to kill or maim her, they would. It was as simple as that.

Kelly dumped her bag and her rackets on the floor and took a quick bath. She needed to relax, to forget all the rubbish in the papers that morning and focus on the match ahead. Only Jessie-Ray Connor stood between her and a Wimbledon final. Win that, and she would be there with the greats. It didn't matter what the papers said, they couldn't take that away from her. She began to clear her mind.

Then there was a scream.

Kelly stood up in the bath just as the door crashed open. Jessie-Ray, half-dressed, looked livid.

"You tried to kill me!" she yelled.

Kelly didn't know what was going on. Then she saw the canister in Jessie-Ray's hand.

"I didn't…"

At that moment, she realized what Jessie-Ray was about to do. Kelly jumped out of the bath just as

Jessie-Ray threw the canister in. There was a sizzling noise, then a little smoke, before the canister sank in the clear water.

"You could have killed me," Kelly said, shocked.

"So," Jessie-Ray snarled, "you admit it."

"It was in my bag," Kelly muttered, almost to herself. "What were you doing going through my bag?"

"You left it on the floor," Jessie-Ray told her. "Deliberately. I stood on it. Oh, you've been very clever, Kelly. You've learnt a lot since you killed Maria. You only injured Louise. Elaine and Lacy got away with fractures and bruises. Me, a mere electric shock."

She held up her foot. Kelly could see where contact with the canister had burnt Jessie-Ray. Was this some kind of elaborate double bluff? Hadn't Jessie-Ray just tried to kill her? The door to the locker-room opened half an inch.

"Five minutes, ladies."

Jessie-Ray kept talking.

"I've got a surprise for you, *lady*. The shock wasn't strong enough. Today, I'm going to slaughter you!"

Feeling unnaturally calm, Kelly began to dry herself.

"We'll see about that," she said.

The two women finished dressing in silence. Then they went out to play.

24

None of Kelly's previous matches had prepared her for appearing on Centre Court at Wimbledon. The court was vast. Kelly felt like she was drowning in a sea of green. There was so much pressure weighing down on her: the tradition, the privilege, the history of the place. And, worst of all, her parents were in the audience. She didn't belong here. But then, neither did Jessie-Ray. Kelly tried to keep her mind focused on the Kipling poem, "If". The whole poem was displayed in the changing rooms so you could read it as you walked out to play.

"If you can keep your head while all around are losing theirs…"

So far, she had kept her head – just. But the toughest part was still to come.

Kelly won the toss and elected to serve. She had a plan and it depended on maintaining a strong serve. Jessie-Ray's first serve was stronger than hers, but usually less accurate. Both players were serve and volleyers, but Jessie-Ray came from an era which still preferred to spend a lot of time at the baseline. Kelly intended to draw her to the net, then play plenty of passing shots.

They finished warming up. Kelly noticed Jessie-Ray whispering to the umpire. Maybe she was telling him about the incident with the canister. Let her. Kelly didn't have time to think about it now. She was about to serve in her first Grand Slam semi-final.

The first game was a gift. Kelly won it to love, but couldn't afford to relax. It was possible that Jessie-Ray was still suffering from her encounter with the anti-mugging device. The older woman held on to her own serve and took Kelly to deuce in the next game. At the crucial point, Kelly produced her first ace. It was going the way she expected. They were testing each other out. It was too early to say who was best placed to win. In many ways, Kelly knew she and Jessie-Ray were evenly matched. In such circumstances, victory either went to the one who wanted it most, or the one who got the lucky breaks.

Jessie-Ray got lucky in the seventh game. As Kelly served for a 4–3 lead at forty-thirty, she broke a string and lost the point. Getting used to the new racket at deuce wasn't easy, and Jessie-Ray broke her. Kelly immediately broke back to love-forty in the next game. Yet, somehow, Jessie-Ray fought back and won what turned out to be the longest game of the match so far. 5-3.

In the change-over, Kelly tried not to get flustered. She was behind, but only just. She could do it. She could…

"Time."

Kelly stood up and served to stay in the set.

She got the first two points, then Jessie-Ray won one back with a brilliant passing shot. Kelly tried to outdo her in the next point with a tight cross-court volley. It went just out.

"Thirty-all."

Kelly cursed herself. It was a rule most players had: never try a really clever shot unless you're two points ahead. She tried to serve an ace but couldn't get it in. Her second serve was short and Jessie-Ray lobbed her. Kelly ran round and got to it but couldn't get the ball back over the net.

"Thirty-forty."

It was break point. Worse, it was set point. Kelly concentrated. She could beat this person. She could. She had to forget that she was serving to stay in the set. All she had to do was play good tennis…

A moment later she was changing ends, having double faulted for the first time in the match. Kelly hung her head. How had she let it go so easily? Now she had a mountain to climb.

"Come on, Kelly!"

"You can do it, Kelly!"

At least there were a few people encouraging her. Kelly recognized the voices of her family and François, but there were others she didn't know: young, urgent, enthusiastic shouters. It seemed that not everybody in England believed all they read in their newspapers. Kelly prepared to receive serve.

With the first set under her belt, Jessie-Ray seemed to relax a little. She was edging ahead, but Kelly kept coming back. At deuce in the third game, Jessie-Ray tried a big serve, and double faulted. Kelly had break point. She knew Jessie-Ray well enough to know that she wouldn't get many chances like this. The next serve was good. Kelly hit it back as low as she could then rushed the net, just as Jessie-Ray's drop shot glided back over. The tiniest of taps, and the game was hers.

Then all hell broke loose. Kelly knew that she only had to hold on to her serve to win the set. Yet Jessie-Ray was intent on competing for every point. Maybe she thought that if it went to a third set, Kelly's extra youth and energy would give her an advantage. Both of them were running all over the court.

Kelly held on to her serve. Jessie-Ray held on to hers. Then the same thing happened again. Kelly could hardly keep track of the score. She no longer found Centre Court intimidating. It was exhilarating. It was the centre of her universe. It was a giant chess-board where she could anticipate every move. Strange how she could only play this well when she was fighting Jessie-Ray.

Because her opponent was equally good. Whatever Kelly threw at her, Jessie-Ray threw right back. Each woman lost points, but neither lost their serve. Balls went out, but by the smallest margin. Each woman seemed to be using every shot that had ever been invented, plus a few which Kelly didn't know the names of. Still they stayed neck and neck – with Kelly's break in the first game keeping her ahead.

After nine games, Kelly was tiring. They had been running non-stop for nearly an hour now. Every game in the set had gone to deuce. The umpire called for new balls. Kelly took the two chilled balls and held one against her forehead, to cool her down. It was only then that she realized she was serving for the set.

She started with an ace. Fifteen-love. A lightning cross-court volley won the next point. Thirty-love. She followed it with her third ace of the match. Forty-love. She had three set points. She went for a fourth ace, but it was just out. Her next serve was deep and Jessie-Ray somehow managed to stay in the rally, shading it at the end. Forty-fifteen. The next rally was even longer. Kelly tried to finish it with a drop shot but the ball refused to go over the net. Forty-thirty. Kelly told herself to be patient. She still had another set point. She served long. Her second serve brushed the net and bounced into the tramlines.

"Deuce."

Kelly couldn't believe her eyes. She'd had three set points. And she'd bottled it. For a few moments, her concentration went. The next thing she knew, it was five games all. The crowd went crazy for Jessie-Ray.

Jessie-Ray won her service game easily. *All right*, thought Kelly. *I'm going to have to take this on the tie-break*. She would show Centre Court what she was made of. She slammed the ball down the centre line.

"Fault!"

Her second serve went in but, as Jessie-Ray returned it, a plane flew overhead. Kelly couldn't hear the sound of the racket hitting the ball, hence was unprepared for the top spin on Jessie-Ray's return. She hit the ball wildly, into the crowd. She won the next point, though, and the one after it. Her confidence returned. Two more points and she was in the tie-break. Jessie-Ray sliced her serve back at her and Kelly went for a safe cross-court return. Too safe. Jessie-Ray was able to volley it out of Kelly's reach.

"Thirty-all."

Kelly tried for an ace, but her arm was tiring and the electric eye beeped her ball out. *Don't let me double fault now*, she told herself. And, of course, because she was thinking about it, she did.

"Thirty-forty."

Jessie-Ray had break point. No, Kelly realized, she had *match point*. This wasn't in her plan at all. People in the crowd were calling, encouraging both players. *I've been really good today*, Kelly thought. *Surely I deserve to win*. But she wasn't sure where she'd get the energy to play another set. Her mind felt drained. How would she face her family if she lost? How would she face François?

"Game, set and match, Mrs Connor. 6-3, 7-5."

Kelly found herself shaking hands with Jessie-Ray. She hadn't even noticed herself double faulting that final service point, throwing the game away. It was over.

"You might be a cheat or a killer," Jessie-Ray said grudgingly, "but you're one hell of a player. You bring out the best in me."

"Ditto," Kelly said.

The crowd applauded long and loud as the two women left the court. *This will be the worst moment*, Kelly thought, *having to sit there with Jessie-Ray*. But the other two players were in there, heartily congratulating the pair of them on playing a fine match. Petra Gordon put an arm round Kelly.

"All that pressure from the papers and you still

nearly cracked it, kid. You'll get there someday, believe me."

Then they were gone and Kelly was on her own. She realized that Jessie-Ray must have gone to do her press conference. There was a knock on the door and Kelly presumed that it would be her parents, or François.

"Come in," she said. "I'm decent."

But it wasn't who she thought it was. Detective Inspector Goad walked into the room, followed by two uniformed officers.

"Miss Christian," she said, "I'm arresting you on the charge of assault and conspiracy to cause grievous bodily harm. You do not have to say anything, but I must warn you that anything you do say will be taken down and may be used in evidence. Do you wish to reply to these charges?"

Behind the inspector, Kelly saw her mother. There was Dad, and her brother, too. A few yards behind them stood François, standing next to Olav. All of them wore sympathetic, hopeful expressions. *I'm hallucinating*, Kelly thought. Mum, not seeing the inspector, spoke:

"We thought we'd give you a few minutes to recover yourself, dear. I know you must feel lousy, but we're really proud of you. You played…"

Then she noticed the inspector, with her grim but triumphant expression.

"What's going on?" Dad asked.

"You'd better collect my semi-finalist's cheque for me," Kelly told her parents. "We're going to need it to pay the lawyers."

"Do you wish to reply to these charges?" the inspector repeated, before Kelly had time to explain any further. One of the other police officers was getting out the handcuffs.

"What's the point?" Kelly told her in a tired voice. "After all, it's obvious that I'm guilty."

4

THE OLD BAILEY

25

Number One court at London's Old Bailey was an even more impressive theatre than Wimbledon's Centre Court, and an even more daunting one. Kelly's opponent this time wasn't one person: it was the whole system. Three weeks had passed since Kelly's Wimbledon semi-final. Another three months would pass before her trial. This was only the committal proceedings. The judge would decide if there was enough evidence for the trial to go ahead.

"Miss Christian was a suspect from the start," Detective Inspector Goad told the court. "In each of the assaults in England, she had the motive and the opportunity. But it was hard to find evidence against her. Miss Christian wasn't questioned about Maria

Hernandez's death by the French police. I spoke to her nearly two weeks later, when it was nearly impossible to check her alibi. Louise Chung survived, but claimed to have no memory of the attack on her. I thought it possible that Miss Chung blocked out this traumatic memory, rather than face the fact that her closest friend was responsible for the fall."

"I object!" Kelly's counsel said. "This is speculation, with not a shred of evidence to back it up. Miss Christian has not been charged with the attempt on Miss Chung's life."

"May I remind you," the judge told the learned QC, "that this is only a preliminary hearing. There's no need to grandstand here. I will decide whether there is enough evidence to proceed to trial. Carry on, Inspector Goad."

The questions continued, every answer incriminating Kelly further. Every thing she had done was shown to have had a suspicious motive. A great deal was made of her sneaking into Jessie-Ray's hotel room. Kelly had been twice photographed wearing disguises. The photographer turned out to have been a fat man in Bermuda shorts that François had several times spotted spying on them. He wasn't a journalist, as Kelly had suspected, but a police photographer.

"What was the purpose of these disguises?" prosecuting counsel asked.

"We suspect that she used disguises when

meeting the person she employed to run over Lacy Cannon."

François wasn't in either photograph. Otherwise they might accuse him, too. But had he been left out deliberately, to make it look like she was meeting someone else? Were they distorting the evidence to get a conviction?

"Objection!" her barrister called, belatedly.

"Perhaps," the judge cautioned, "you could speculate a little less, Inspector, and move on to what evidence you do have."

Prosecuting counsel asked for permission to call exhibit three. The anti-mugging device was brought into evidence. The prosecution, of course, made a meal of it. Kelly couldn't stand it. She blanked the court room out. She had to keep her head clear for when she gave evidence herself. That was, presuming her counsel called her at all. Her QC was worried that, every time Kelly opened her mouth, she incriminated herself further. The main evidence against her, after all, was the confession Kelly had made in the locker-room at Wimbledon.

Kelly was lucky. She had enough money to get out on bail and employ a QC – Queen's Counsel – one of the best barristers in Britain. If the case went to full trial, she didn't know what she would do. They had some kind of legal aid scheme here, but Kelly doubted whether it applied to Americans. All of her prize money was gone. Her sponsors had dropped her like a hot brick as soon as she was arrested. Her tennis career was effectively over. The only issue that remained was whether she'd spend the next ten or so years of her life in jail.

At least François had stuck with her. Kelly's boyfriend had been in court every day. Banned from the Wimbledon grounds, she missed him winning the boys' Junior tournament. His victory made her feel immensely proud of him. But the papers the next day managed to soil his achievement. They weren't interested in the tennis, only in the fact that François was Kelly's boyfriend.

After Inspector Goad, Mary appeared to give evidence. The coach had stuck by Kelly. Kelly's arrest meant that Mary was out of a job, but never once had Mary suggested that Kelly might be guilty. Kelly wouldn't be surprised if Mary suspected it. In the witness box, Kelly's former coach tried her best to defend her star pupil.

"This mysterious motorcyclist. Did you see his first appearance, Miss Porter?"

"No. But that doesn't mean anything. The second time was real enough."

"I put it to you, Miss Porter, that the second so-called attack was no more real than the first. I suggest that you and Miss Christian invented the second attack to make it appear that Kelly was in danger."

"Nonsense."

"That's not a direct reply, Miss Porter. After all, the attack was conveniently timed, wasn't it? The press were attacking Miss Christian for the incident where she 'fell' into Elaine Murdoch…"

Mary looked pained. She didn't like the court room and her discomfort was obvious.

"When did Kelly tell you about the first attack?"

"Kelly told me about the first motorbike attack a few days afterwards. I believe she told Andrew shortly after it happened."

"What reason did she have for keeping quiet about this incident?"

"I don't know."

"You, the person on the tour closest to her, don't know? Does it occur to you, Miss Porter, that your protégée might have made this story up?"

"No. I've never known Kelly to tell an untruth, so I assumed…"

The counsel interrupted.

"You've never known her to tell an untruth? But according to your testimony earlier, Kelly Christian was stringing two boyfriends along during the Wimbledon period. How did she manage this without telling … untruths?"

"It wasn't like that…"

"Where was Kelly when Maria Hernandez was killed, Miss Porter?"

"In the hotel with me. Then we took a taxi together…"

The counsel shook his head.

"According to witnesses we've just tracked down, you didn't join Kelly in the lobby until ten minutes *after* Miss Hernandez met her death. Do you know what she was doing immediately before that?"

"No, but I'm sure … eh…"

"Has Kelly Christian ever asked you to fake an alibi for her, Miss Porter?"

"No."

"Did you see her being given the assault weapon by her brother?"

"No."

"Did you know that Kelly was taking the canister into the changing-rooms with her?"

"No, I would have warned her against doing so. It was a silly mistake."

"At least you admit that your protégée is capable of mistakes."

By the time she left the witness box, Mary was in tears. Kelly felt sorrier for her than she did for herself.

Peter Kong gave his evidence next. Kelly hadn't got round to returning his calls until after she was arrested. When she did call, the millionaire refused to speak to her. He had withdrawn Olav, the bodyguard. Kelly should have made efforts to be nice to him earlier. Instead, she had snubbed the millionaire, despite the favours he had done for her. He would not be a favourable witness but, smartly dressed and completely relaxed, he made a compellingly credible one.

"Tell us about the day of Louise Chung's accident," the prosecution asked.

"I knew that Louise was going for a walk. She wanted to be alone. Later, I noticed Kelly following her. I was ... suspicious. I followed the girls myself, at a distance. About half an hour later, I practically bumped into Kelly, running away from the accident. She made up some story about seeing Louise on the beach below. She seemed very distressed. At the time, I believed her completely. Now, it's obvious to me that Kelly tried to kill Louise. She made up the story about running for help because bumping into me spoiled her plan."

"I object!"

But Kelly's QC was too late. The damage had already been done.

"You provided her with a bodyguard, I believe."

"Yes. I was concerned for her safety. But she kept refusing."

"Why do you think that was?"

"Objection!"

"Sustained."

"I'll change the question. When did Kelly accept your offer of the bodyguard?"

"After the second so-called motorbike attack."

When Kong was through, Elaine Murdoch testified. She was not responsible, Kelly had found out, for the food poisoning at Edgbaston. A careless caterer was. But Elaine claimed that Kelly was responsible for her broken ankle, and it was hard to prove otherwise.

Next was the new Wimbledon Ladies' singles champion, Jessie-Ray Connor, who told how Kelly had deliberately left her bag where the champion was bound to step on it and activate the anti-mugging device. Then she was asked about finding Kelly in her room.

"I don't know what she was trying to do. She told the police some stupid story about perfume. Maybe she was going to set up some kind of accident, or plant some drugs in my bag then call the police. I dread to think."

Finally, Lacy Cannon described the motorcyclist who had knocked her over. Then she added, with the voice of bitter experience:

"You know, until Kelly walked into my bedroom that afternoon, I still wasn't sure about her. But then she had the nerve to say the same thing had happened to her the day before. I mean – give me credit for some intelligence, you know? She was adding insult to injury."

"Put me in the witness box," Kelly pleaded with her QC.

The counsel shook her head.

"They'd make mincemeat of you, Kelly. Leave this to me. Ours isn't like the American system. No court room pyrotechnics. If I'm going to get you off, you have to let me do it my way."

The defence lasted less than three minutes.

"There is no case to answer," the QC told the judge. "The case against my client is entirely circumstantial. I can't imagine why the Crown Prosecution Service brought this to court. Presumably, they were put under pressure by the enormous amount of publicity the attacks on tennis stars have received. As it is, a young woman has been put under enormous stress. I don't propose to place her under further stress by putting her in the witness box today."

There was an audible groan from the press area. The Queen's Counsel paused for it to die down before continuing her speech.

"For all the nonsense talked today, the prosecution case rests on one point, and one point alone – my client's so-called confession. Inspector Goad took Kelly's words to mean that she confessed to all of the charges against her. But the other people in the room – people who knew her well, her own family – will testify at full trial that Kelly's words were ironic. Listen to those words again. 'What's the point?' Kelly asked. 'After all, it's obvious that I'm guilty.'

"This is an intelligent girl, your honour. She's tired. She's just lost the biggest, most prestigious sporting battle of her life. Yet she still comes up with a rhetorical question which implies, not guilt, but cynicism about the judicial process: 'What's the point?'

"Next, she makes a sarcastic remark: 'After all, it's obvious that I'm guilty.' Maybe her humour here is questionable. Or maybe her sarcasm is apt. The police seemed determined to arrest someone for these terrible crimes against tennis players. Kelly knew that she was what Americans call 'the fall guy'.

"You cannot commit this girl to trial for the crimes she is charged with. Even the – admitted – incident with the anti-mugging device was an accident, not an assault. The only person in any danger was Kelly herself, when her opponent threw the canister into her bath water. True, possession of the canister was illegal, but Kelly wasn't to know that. Her brother explained to the police how he brought it over from America without his sister's knowledge.

"Until two months ago, this young woman had an incredibly promising career. Now, her life has been ruined, while a dangerous killer goes free. Kelly has not been charged with the murder of Maria Hernandez, and the evidence for her involvement in the attack on Louise Chung is laughable – the conjecture of a rich man whose advances Kelly spurned until she needed his protection from a genuine threat.

"Kelly's only crime has been to try to find the real culprit, the person who nearly killed her best friend. It's even possible that this villain was somebody who gave evidence in the court room today. I don't know. What I do know is that this isn't a question of reasonable doubt. It's a matter of fact. There isn't a shred of evidence against Kelly Christian.

"You have to let her go."

The judge reserved his decision until the next day and they all went home.

Kelly spent her last evening of freedom with François. Her boyfriend was about to start his studies at the Sorbonne. To take their minds off her troubles, Kelly tried to get François to talk about himself. It disturbed her that her boyfriend was giving up tennis.

"Won't you play some tournaments in the vacations at least?"

François shook his head.

"Not yet. Tennis can wait," he said. "Maybe I could make a good living, but what's happened to you has taken away my taste for it. I want a life outside tennis, a life of the mind, not just the body. Only education can give me that. Maybe, in three years, I'll be ready to play professionally. Or maybe I'll have given it up altogether. Who knows? Who cares?"

"I do," Kelly said.

They embraced, then went downstairs to eat a last meal with Kelly's family. Would François wait for her if she went to prison? Kelly didn't dare ask. When she got out, they'd be about twenty-eight years old. It was impossible to imagine what kind of person they would both be by then. British prisons were thought to be amongst the worst in Europe. Who knew what the experience might turn Kelly into?

In court the next day, there were no tennis stars waiting for the judge's decision. Only Mary was present. Louise sent a telegram wishing Kelly luck, but she was still on crutches and couldn't travel. Kelly guessed that Louise's sponsors had warned her not to be seen supporting her old friend. Kelly couldn't blame her for not coming. Maybe Louise even thought that Kelly was the one who pushed her off the cliff. Kelly didn't know anything about anyone any more.

The judge's speech was brief and to the point.

"The prosecution has failed to show that there is a case to answer. All of the evidence they have produced is circumstantial. Miss Murdoch's injury was an accident, not an assault. The defendant was equally likely to have been injured herself. The only charge which Miss Christian has to answer is that involving the electric canister. But the stress which these proceedings has already taken on her far exceeds any punishment that she might receive for this offence."

Kelly wasn't sure she understood all of what he'd said. But she understood the next part, as the judge turned to her and said:

"You are free to go."

There was uproar in the court. François embraced her, then Kelly ran into the arms of her family. The QC, helped by three police officers, bundled Kelly out of the court, where a mob of media personnel awaited her.

"It wasn't a complete success," the QC told Kelly. "The judge didn't say anything about there not being a stain on your character. And they can bring charges again, but only if there's substantial new evidence."

"Thank you," Kelly said. "Thanks for everything."

The QC shook Kelly's hand but didn't meet her eyes. *She thinks I'm guilty*, Kelly realized. *She did her job, but she still thinks I did it*. As they left the court, Kelly brushed by Detective Inspector Goad.

"You got away with it," she said, smiling resignedly.

Kelly hurried by without replying.

The QC gave a brief statement to the press, saying that Kelly felt vindicated and asking them to leave her alone. As Kelly got into the car, she had endless notes thrust at her, each offering thousands and thousands of pounds to tell her side of the story in one of the tabloid papers. Kelly threw them all away. She'd rather go bankrupt than let those creeps contaminate her life any further.

Kelly knew how it would be reported in the press the next day. The press wouldn't be allowed to say that she was guilty, but they wouldn't concede that Kelly might be innocent either. She no longer cared what people said about her. The public life was meaningless. What counted was the opinion of her friends and family. What counted was being able to live with yourself.

That night, Kelly went out for a meal with François and her family, who were flying back to Boston the next day. Kelly was going to spend some time with François's family in France, away from the English-speaking media. On their way back to the hotel, they passed a stand selling early editions of the next day's papers. They were even worse than Kelly had expected. The press had a new story.

"BANNED! FREED STAR CAN'T PLAY TENNIS FOR THREE YEARS!"

It seemed that the International Tennis Association had met immediately after the trial and agreed to prohibit Kelly from playing in any tournaments for the next three years. The reason they gave was the only offence that she'd admitted: taking an illegal anti-mugging device into the Wimbledon locker-room.

"It's outrageous!" François said. "You have to challenge it!"

"How?" Kelly asked him. "I've no money left to pay lawyers with."

Kelly didn't see her parents off at the airport. There would be too many journalists waiting to harass her. Kelly wasn't travelling by plane herself. She and François were taking the ferry from Portsmouth to St Malo the next day, Sunday. There, they would meet François's family and explore the French countryside. By the time the press found out Kelly had gone, it would be too late to find her.

It was their last day in London, a city Kelly hoped never to see again. She and François decided to go to Notting Hill and explore the Portobello Road. Kelly hadn't felt like acting the tourist since she'd been arrested. To be honest, she didn't really feel like it now. However, François was keen, and she had nothing better to do. She tied her hair back with a rubber band and put on her ugly, plain-lensed, plastic glasses. She now had half a dozen pairs of plain glasses and as many scruffy hair-styles. The disguise seemed to work.

Portobello Road was buzzing. The young couple dodged in and out of antique shops, junk shops, book shops, comic shops and record shops. François wanted to buy presents for his parents and his younger sister. Kelly found the people on the street more interesting than the inside of the shops. So, while François looked in a place called *Books for Cooks*, she stood on the path outside, watching the world go by. Then someone shouted at her.

"Look out!"

Kelly span round. A motorbike had mounted the pavement and was heading straight towards her. *Surely*, she thought, *not here, in front of so many people?* It was the same bike, the same rider hidden behind the same helmet. She hadn't been able to describe it to the police, but she recognized it now.

The bike pulled up a few inches from Kelly. The rider smiled and took off his helmet.

"I thought it was you," he said. "I've been looking for you all over London. I wanted one last look before you left."

"This is me," Kelly said softly, still a little unsteady on her feet.

"You got off," the young man said, in the soft, Scottish accent she had once been so fond of. "Congratulations."

"Thank you."

"Don't worry," Andrew added with a malicious grin. "I won't tell." He put his helmet back on and revved up the bike.

"Wait," Kelly said. "I want to know why…"

But Andrew Kerr was gone, speeding off to God knew where. A moment later, François came out of the shop, proudly holding up a book by Raymond Blanc.

"You can't get this in France," he said. "Hey! What's wrong? You're white as a sheet."

"We'd better go to the nearest police station," Kelly said. "I don't know how, or even why, but I think I've found out who really did it."

5

US OPEN
FOUR YEARS LATER

Epilogue

Helicopters hovered over Manhattan. Kelly could see them from her twelfth-floor window, in the narrow crack of light which made its way down between the tall buildings. She switched on the air conditioning. The roar was so loud that she couldn't hear the TV. Paint peeled from the brown walls of the room. This hotel was a far cry from the ones she'd stayed in when she was a tennis star, but it didn't bother her. Those days were gone. Maybe there'd be other days. Maybe not.

Returning to America wasn't easy. Kelly had avoided doing it for so many years, despite her family's frequent complaints. They couldn't afford to visit her in Europe more than once a year. But Kelly wasn't ready to go back. At first, the TV networks kept offering her money. They wanted to make a mini-series, or a TV movie about her life. But Kelly never returned their calls. Eventually, they gave up. To support her education, Kelly did part-time jobs: shop assistant, sales person, cleaner, cashier … she even worked in the Paris Burger King, until, one day, somebody recognized her.

"Aren't you…?"

But that was two years ago. Now, she was more or less forgotten. It was time to start again. Kelly felt like a different person from the one she'd been at seventeen. She was twenty-two in three weeks' time. She was a grown-up. And, anyhow, she missed the States. Nowhere in Europe could give you the same buzz as New York. And the three weeks she'd spent in Nahant, catching up with family and friends, had been wonderful. When she left New York she was going to stay with Louise at her beach house in Malibu.

It was mid-morning and the hotel was quiet. Kelly left her room. She wanted to pick up some things from the pharmacy before brunch. She was about to call the lift when she heard a door opening and a familiar voice called her.

"Kelly, is that really you?" Mary Porter asked. "Kelly Christian?"

Kelly turned and nodded. It was the first time she'd been recognized since arriving in New York. Memories faded fast.

"Short hair suits you."

The two women hugged each other.

"What are you doing here?" Kelly asked her former coach.

"I have a new protégée," Mary said.

Kelly noticed the tennis racket in Mary's hand. It was made by the same company who had briefly sponsored Kelly.

"She's a fifteen-year-old," Mary went on. "Very talented."

"That's great."

Kelly and Mary had lost touch. She felt ambivalent about seeing her former coach again. They had been very close for a long time. Yet, looking back, Mary had tried to turn Kelly into something she never wanted to become: a cynical, single-minded, unscrupulous success. Kelly knew that the years since the trial hadn't been good for Mary. The former champion lost all of her commentating work and was reduced to coaching at clubs – not even the larger ones. She must be knocking forty now, but looked a lot older. Kelly had also heard rumours that Mary had been hospitalized for depression. It was good to see her back.

"Are you playing?" Mary asked.

"Kind of," Kelly said. "I'm in the qualifiers. And I'm in the mixed doubles with François. Oh, by the way, it's not Kelly Christian any more. It's Madame Mersault."

She held up her wedding-ring for Mary to see.

"We married as soon as François graduated."

"That's wonderful. Congratulations. So you're a French citizen now?"

Kelly smiled.

"That's right. I've been playing in a few tournaments since I finished my degree this summer. Most people don't remember the stories about me. And those who do remember don't seem to care. I'm more comfortable there."

"They'll forgive you here, too," Mary said. "They forgave Jessie-Ray."

"True," Kelly said. "People will always forgive success."

Since winning Wimbledon four years earlier, Jessie-Ray had returned to the top ranks of women's tennis. She was currently the world number three, behind Sue Murray and Louise Chung. Elaine Murdoch was currently number eleven. Lacy Cannon had had a more chequered career since splitting with her original coach, Chuck Dexter. She'd made the top ten two years before, but had recently retired from the game to concentrate on raising a family. She had twin girls by her handsome young husband, a rock musician.

"You know," Kelly said to Mary, as they waited for the lift to come, "there's one thing I always meant to ask you."

Mary smiled.

"Don't tell me. You want to know how I put the extra back spin on those low cross-court returns."

"That too," Kelly said. "But no, I wanted to know why you got rid of François in Paris that time. Remember?"

Mary frowned.

"Not really. You say I *got rid* of him … how?"

"After I got knocked out of the third round, he disappeared. I thought he'd gone off me. Then, when we got back together, François told me that he came looking for me after the game in Paris. But he found you instead. And you told him that I wasn't interested. That I'd only been using him as a hitting partner. He was pretty hurt. He won the tournament, but I wasn't there to see him win. Why did you do it, Mary?"

The former star looked embarrassed.

"It was so long ago," she said. "I'm not sure I really remember. If I did do as your husband said, I'm sure it was for your own good. But I can't remember why. I'm sorry if it hurt you."

"Apology accepted," Kelly said. "I guessed you were trying to protect my tennis. I remember how you warned me off Andrew Kerr, too."

"Oh, yes," Mary said. "Andrew. Whatever happened to him?"

Kelly didn't answer directly.

"You know, I was convinced for a while that Andrew was the person behind all the attacks."

"That's ridiculous," Mary commented in a shrill voice.

"Not really," Kelly said. "I told the police what I knew after my trial, but I don't think they investigated it seriously."

"Did you see Andrew again?"

"Only briefly."

Mary nodded distractedly.

"You haven't stayed in touch?"

"Andrew died in a motorbike accident," Kelly told her, "in his second term at university."

"How tragic," Mary said, though she didn't look upset. "But, you know, he always was a maniac on that motorbike."

"I guess," Kelly said. She paused, then added, "I'm sure that he was involved in some way. The last time we met, he more or less admitted it to me."

Mary took Kelly's arm.

"You must put all of that behind you, dear. We'll never be sure who was responsible – what was deliberate, and what was an accident."

"I guess you're right," Kelly said. "But it bugs me. Here I am, starting to play tennis again, and some of my suspects are still around on the circuit: Peter Kong, Elaine, Jessie-Ray…"

Suddenly, it was as though a switch had clicked in her mind and a light come on. Kelly felt dizzy for a moment. She tried to stay calm.

"You used to see Andrew on his motorbike, you say?"

Mary looked puzzled, then concerned. The lift arrived and she pressed the hold button.

"I think I saw him riding it once or twice."

"You see," Kelly said, "I never saw him on it – at least, not knowing that it was him – not until my very last day in London."

"What are you trying to say?" Mary wanted to know.

"I know that Andrew didn't commit most of the attacks on tennis players. He wasn't in Paris, and he was taking an exam when Louise fell off the cliff. I checked. But I think that it was him who tried to run me over in Eastbourne. I know that he came to London a day earlier than he was meant to, I checked that too. So I think it was him who tried to run me over there. And I think it was him who fractured Lacy Cannon's arm."

"But what motive would he have?" Mary asked.

"That's what I could never quite figure out," Kelly told her. "At first, I thought it was jealousy. But both times he rode at me were before he knew about François. When did you say you saw him on his motorbike?"

"Er…"

Kelly pressed her point.

"Because, you see, I never even knew he had a motorbike. Nor did his parents, not until he came back from Eastbourne on it. He told them a girl-friend had bought it for him. They assumed it was me. But it wasn't. I told them so at his funeral. They had no idea who else it could be. I thought he must have bought it himself, with the money we paid him for being my hitting partner."

"I guess that was it," Mary said.

"But that would be nowhere near enough money," Kelly went on. "Unless he was being paid for other services, too, some things I didn't know about…"

The lift made a beeping noise. Someone else had called it. As the lift went up and the outer doors began to shut, Mary shoved the tennis racket she was carrying between the doors, stopping them from closing completely. Kelly trembled.

"You're right," Mary said quietly. "I did pay for that motorbike."

"But why? Why did you get him to try to run me over?"

Mary laughed – a dry, peculiar laugh.

"He never tried to run *you* over. It was only meant to look like that. I got the idea from the accident Sue Murray had. The first time, I told Andrew that you needed a scare to motivate you. It worked, didn't it?"

Kelly nodded.

"I guess. And the second time?"

"After the on-court incident with Elaine, we

needed something which would put you back in public favour, something to direct suspicion away from you. But it backfired. There were no witnesses and people accused us of making it up."

"And he was the one who knocked Lacy over, too?" Kelly asked.

Mary nodded the way she did when her pupil had finally grasped an elementary point.

"It was hard persuading him to do that. Andrew had just found out about François. I persuaded him that the way back into your good books was to help you win your match. When I saw him afterwards I told him that it hadn't worked. That must have been when he went to the tabloids with his little kiss-and-tell story. He wasn't very bright."

The lift door was still jammed open. Kelly pretended that she hadn't noticed. Her pulse was racing, but she needed to play dumb to find out the full story.

"I don't understand about the perfume," she said to Mary.

Mary hesitated, but seemed to decide that she might as well finish what she'd started. She gripped Kelly's arm tightly.

"Jessie-Ray always used that perfume," Mary explained. "It was her I wanted to incriminate. I'd seen what you were capable of in France. With Hernandez dead and Murray out of the way, Louise and Jessie-Ray were your only serious rivals. So I daubed myself with Baudelaire before following Louise that afternoon. She made it easy for me by climbing on to the cliff. I disguised myself, but no one spotted me, not even you. There was a risk that Louise would turn and see me, of course, but I didn't expect her to survive. That wasn't in the plan. I hoped that the police forensics team would find traces of the perfume on the body when they did the inquest. But Louise survived and the stupid English police didn't even do the tests."

"But why did you do all this?" Kelly wanted to know. "Why?"

Mary's voice became urgent, almost warm.

"I did it for you, Kelly. You had it in you to be a great champion, the one I should have been. I was never ruthless enough. But I was teaching you to be hard, and I was ruthless for you. You see, you need to make it while you're young. Look at me. I never won a Grand Slam final, and no one remembers my name. My best chance was the year Jessie-Ray beat me in the Wimbledon semis.

"Do you know what Jessie-Ray did two nights before that match? She stole my boyfriend, Rob Baker. We'd been together nearly a year."

Kelly had heard of Baker. He was a former top ten player.

"I didn't know that you and he were involved."

"That year at Wimbledon, Jessie picked Rob up, slept with him, then made sure I knew about it. We broke up the day of the semi-final. I was a mess. I lost against Jessie and I kept losing. But I got back at her. Maybe my game went to hell because of it, but I put all my energy into thwarting her.

"You see, in the season before I retired, I sneaked into Jessie's room two different times, and planted drugs there. Then I gave the police an anonymous tip-off. Later, Jessie got into drugs for real, but she has me to thank for starting her off." Mary laughed angrily. "If things had gone according to plan, I'd have finished her off, too."

Her voice became less bitter, more philosophical.

"I so much wanted you to beat her in that semi, Kelly, to do it for me. You were good enough. But you blew it. You'll never get that far again."

If that's the price of victory, Kelly thought, *I don't want it.* She didn't tell Mary this. Her former coach was clearly deranged.

"I did it all for you, Kelly," Mary went on. "I took all those risks so that you'd take my revenge for me. And it nearly worked. You beat Jessie-Ray once, and you could have done it again. If you hadn't taken that stupid weapon into the locker-room, you'd have won Wimbledon. You know that, don't you?"

"But it wouldn't have been fair, would it?" Kelly couldn't stop herself saying. "Not after you'd killed Maria, then maimed Louise and Lacy."

Mary didn't deny murdering Hernandez.

"*Fair?*" she sneered. "Was it fair that my career

ended when I was thirty? What's fairness got to do with tennis? Nothing. Nothing at all."

"Anyway," Kelly said, glancing over Mary's shoulder down the empty hotel corridor, "your secret's safe with me. I won't tell."

"That's good," Mary said. "I was sorry for all you had to go through, but, like I explained, it was your own fault. My new girl – she'll go all the way. I'm sure of it."

"Good luck," Kelly said, beginning to back away from Mary.

She tried to loosen her arm from Mary's grip.

"Oh, I make my own luck," Mary said. "It's the only kind you can trust."

With that, she pressed the lift button on the wall and swung her whole body round, throwing Kelly towards the lift shaft. Kelly screamed, then began to fall.

"I'm sorry I have to do this, Kelly," Mary said, thrusting Kelly into the darkness.

Kelly felt her legs dangling over emptiness.

Then Mary let go.

But Kelly didn't let Mary go. If she was going to die, she would take this killer with her. She clung on to Mary's right arm. The coach tried to tear Kelly off her. There was a noise from above, but Kelly ignored it.

"Help!" she shouted.

Mary nearly over-balanced. She was having to

use one arm to hold on to the wall while she tried to shake Kelly off her other arm. The noise above Kelly grew louder. Without looking up, she realized what it was.

"Pull me out!" she shouted. "Pull me out before it kills both of us!"

Mary responded by kicking Kelly so hard that she nearly lost her grip. Above them, the lift hurtled down.

"Help!" Kelly screamed again. Once more, Mary's foot crashed into her stomach.

"Kelly!"

The next thing Kelly knew, there were arms round her chest. Both she and Mary were being pulled back from the brink. The lift shot by, jarring Kelly's arm as her husband pulled the two women clear.

"What happened?" François asked. "Was it an accident?"

"There's no such thing as an accident," Mary said as the lift doors began to close once more.

She stepped through the doors. Kelly, still in shock, assumed that the lift had returned. Maybe Mary thought the same thing. But François, realizing what was happening, reached out to stop Mary. He was too late. The doors shut. A fraction of a second later, they heard a dull thud.

"It was her," François said. "It was her all along, wasn't it?"

"Yes."

Kelly reached for her husband. He held her very close. After a minute or two, the young couple walked down to the lobby, where they would tell their story to the police, then begin the rest of their lives.

On the twelfth floor, a fifteen-year-old girl left her room, carrying a heavy equipment bag. She was heading downstairs to the lobby, where she would join her tennis coach. The girl had come to compete in the Junior section of the US Open tournament. It was her first time in New York and she was very excited.

When she got to the elevator, the girl was surprised to come across her coach's tennis racket. It lay, discarded, beside the lift doors. The expensive racket appeared to be undamaged. On closer examination, however, it turned out to have a hairline crack in the handle which made it dangerous to use. The girl picked the racket up and put it into her bag with the others. Then she pressed the button which called the elevator.

But the elevator didn't come.

P●INT CRiME

A murder has been committed... Whodunnit?
An exciting series of crime novels, with tortuous
plots and lots of suspects, designed to keep you
guessing until the very last page.

Other Point Crime titles by David Belbin:

AVENGING ANGEL
Traffic's murder tonight...

FINAL CUT
Lights, camera ... murder...

SHOOT THE TEACHER
Even teachers don't deserve to die...

Also by David Belbin:

Life on the beat isn't always easy ...
Discover some of the problems young police
officers face with *The Beat*, the gripping new
crime series set in an inner city police station.

MISSING PERSON
*Hannah Brown's just another fifteen-year-old
runaway, isn't she? Only PC Clare Coppola
doesn't think so...*

Look out for:

BLACK AND BLUE
*It's not always easy for Ben being a black
police officer. Especially when there seems to
be racial trouble brewing on his beat...*